Mrs. Viola Piercey
314 Verdun Dr.
Clarksville, TN 37042-4250

D0886872

By E. X. Ferrars

Root of All Evil

Root of All Evil

E. X. FERRARS

PUBLISHED FOR THE CRIME CLUB BY
DOUBLEDAY & COMPANY, INC.
GARDEN CITY, NEW YORK
1984

All of the characters in this book
are fictitious, and any resemblance
to actual persons, living or dead,
is purely coincidental.

Library of Congress Cataloging in Publication Data
Ferrars, E. X.
Root of all evil.
I. Title.
PR6003.R458R6   1984   823'.912
ISBN 0-385-19580-X
Library of Congress Catalog Card Number 84-6086

First Edition in the United States of America

Root of All Evil

CHAPTER ONE

"Andrew?" the voice on the telephone said. "This is Felicity."

Felicity. Surely a voice from the dead.

"Yes?" Andrew Basnett said confusedly.

"Felicity Silvester." The voice was sharper.

"Oh yes, of course, Felicity," Andrew said. "I'm sorry, the telephone woke me out of a nap. I was muddled for a moment."

"What are you doing, having a nap at your age at this time of day?" the voice asked.

"I'm seventy, Felicity."

"A mere child. I'm eighty-five."

"And how are you?"

"Better than you might expect. Still reasonably mobile and suffering only occasionally from attacks of senility."

"I'm delighted to hear it."

"Andrew, it's a very long time since we last saw each other."

"Yes, it's a very long time. Four years, is it? Five years?"

"Don't bother trying to tot it up. What's a year or two here or there at my age? I saw you at poor Nell's funeral and that's ten years ago and you've been down to visit me once or twice since then. But now I'd like to see you again, Andrew. I've reached an age when I want to see all my really old friends at least once more. Suppose you come and spend Easter with me."

Felicity Silvester had never really been a friend of Andrew's. She was a cousin of Nell's, Andrew's wife, who had died ten years ago of cancer. Nell, so Andrew had believed, had never been particularly fond of Felicity, but she had had a great capacity for loyalty to her numerous relations, and if Nell would have thought that Andrew should spend Easter with Felicity, he was prepared to do so.

"Thank you," he said. "That's a most attractive suggestion. But won't it be rather a lot of trouble for you? Suppose I come just for the day."

"It's no trouble at all," Felicity replied. "I've still got my wonderful Mrs. Cavell, who manages everything for me, and I've blossomed out recently into a manservant. You remember Agnes Cavell, of course."

"I'm not sure I do," Andrew said.

"No, come to think of it, she may have come to me since your last visit. And that dates it, because Agnes has been with me for four years. I know that, because we were talking about it only the other day. So it must be nearly five years since we've seen each other. Well, you'll come for Easter, won't you, Andrew?"

"Yes, thank you very much, Felicity."

"Come on Thursday. You don't want to travel on Good Friday—there aren't any trains to speak of. Come in the morning. There's a good train that gets here about twelve thirty-five. Then take a taxi. I won't send Laycock to meet you with the car, because you and he won't know each other. Laycock's the manservant I mentioned. Don't you think there's something rather grand about having a manservant these days?"

"Very grand," Andrew said.

"I wish I could call him my butler. I've always wanted to have a butler. My grandfather had one when I was a child, and I adored him. I liked him ever so much better than my grandfather. But Laycock just wouldn't shape up to it, though he does his best. Well, I'll expect you on Thursday about one o'clock. I'm so glad you're coming. Of course Derek and Frances will be here and for once the children too, so you won't have to put up with too much of me. Good-bye, Andrew."

"Good-bye, Felicity. Thank you so much for asking me."

Putting the telephone down, Andrew wondered who on earth Derek and Frances were and to whom the children mentioned by Felicity belonged. Faintly the names Derek and Frances rang a bell. He thought that perhaps if they were relations of Nell's, she might have spoken of them at some time. But unfortunately the names did not evoke any memory of faces to go with them. Not that that meant so very much. His memory, he was only too well aware, was deteriorating rapidly.

That did not apply to the events of his youth. He had astonishingly vivid recollections of his childhood. Yet the face and the name of someone whom he had met only a week before might be wiped clean from his memory almost in minutes. He would have been the worst possible sort of witness at a trial, he had often thought. He might actually have watched a murder being committed and afterwards would have been unable to say whether the murderer had been tall or short, dark or fair, well dressed or in dirty jeans. Even books that he had read only two or three weeks ago and in which he had been really interested soon faded into a grey blur unless he had made careful notes while he was reading.

Notes. That reminded him . . .

He had intended to spend the afternoon going over the notes that he had made yesterday in the library of the Royal Society in connection with the life that he was writing of Robert Hooke, the noted seventeenth-century natural philosopher, but instead he had fallen into the sleep from which Felicity's telephone call had roused him. But now that he was fully awake he could get ahead with some work.

A slight reluctance to do so kept him extended on the sofa for a little while, but taking a firm grip on himself, he got up and padded across the room in his socks to the desk where his

papers were heaped up in what to anyone but himself would
have been incomprehensible disorder. On his way he stumbled
over a pair of slippers that were lying in the middle of the
room. He very seldom wore slippers or shoes when he was
alone in his flat in St. John's Wood, but preferred to wander
around in his socks, leaving the slippers lying wherever they
had happened to fall when he kicked them off. As he went he
declaimed:

> "When all the world is young, lad,
>   And all the trees are green;
>   And every goose a swan, lad,
>   And every lass a queen . . ."

Annoyed with himself, he tried to stop, but even though he
silenced his tongue, the words went relentlessly on in his head.
He had been haunted by the verse all day. It was not that he
was suffering from an attack of nostalgia for his own departed
youth, but he had always been given to reciting to himself,
aloud if there was no one else in the flat, and it happened that
when he had been eleven or so and at the height of his powers
for learning verse by heart, he had had a passion for Kingsley.
He had also venerated Newbolt and Kipling, and as a result
had had to endure a fair amount of torment on their account
in later years. He had done his best to oust them by memo-
rizing Shakespeare, Milton, Donne and others from whom he
would have continued to derive genuine pleasure, but the impressions made by his early enthusiasms went too deep to be
effaced and nearly always triumphed.

> "Then hey for boot and horse, lad,
>   And round the world away . . ."

Frowning, he sat down, drew towards him the papers he
wanted and at last, as he lost himself in facts and figures,
succeeded in banishing the tiresome jingle.

He had been writing his book on Robert Hooke for three

years. Sometimes he felt that there was strangely little to show
for so many hours of work, spread over such a long time, but
the truth was that as he went along he kept on tearing up
almost as much as he wrote. At the back of his mind there
lurked a fear that perhaps the book would never be finished.
And perhaps the truth was that he did not really want to finish
it, for it had kept him occupied in a reasonably contented way
ever since his retirement and he did not know what he would
do with himself once it was done.

The first year after his retirement from the chair of botany
in one of London University's many colleges he had spent
going round the world, lecturing in the United States, New
Zealand, Australia and India, and he had found that very en-
joyable. But after his return home, life would have been very
empty for him and the loneliness that he had felt ever since
Nell's death would have been intolerable if he had not committed himself to work of some sort.

He did not look forward much to his visit to Felicity Silvester. He knew that she would make him comfortable. She was a
rich woman and her home on the outskirts of the small town
of Braden-on-Thames was luxurious. But as he remembered
her, she had been an arrogant woman, charming and entertaining when she felt in the mood to be so, but difficult if she
ever felt that her dominance was being challenged. Nell had
always said of her that she was kind and generous and that the
trouble with her was simply that when she was young she had
been a great beauty and so had become accustomed, simply on
account of it, to having her own way. She had been married to
a husband twenty years older than herself, who had adored her
and who had been what was to Andrew that most mysterious
of mammals, Something in the City. Whatever it was that
James Silvester had done in the City, he had left his widow,
when he died at the age of sixty-five, a considerable fortune.
Andrew remembered that she had sent Nell and him a sump-
tuous wedding present of Georgian silver, and for a time, since

she had been living in London then, they had seen a good deal
of her. But after a few years she had moved to Braden-on-
Thames, which was because . . .

Ah yes. Andrew's memory, as he sat looking at his notes,
suddenly became active. She had moved to be near her son,
Derek. Derek was a doctor in Braden-on-Thames and Frances
was his wife. That was who they were. And Andrew had a
vague belief that they had children, though how many of them
there were or of what ages they might be now he had no idea.
The thought of their presence did not add to the attractions of
his visit. He had become very tired of the young in his last
years of trying to teach them. Probably it had been his own
fault, but it had come to seem to him that they all displayed a
dreadful similarity to one another, and by degrees he had become convinced that real individuality, of the kind in which he
could still feel interested, was to be found only in children
under twenty months and in men and women over thirty.

The Thursday morning on which he set off for Braden-on-
Thames was April at its most cheerless, bleak and blustery,
with only an occasional glint of blue showing itself halfheart-
edly through the hurrying clouds. He took a taxi to Paddington, arriving there as he always did at any station, anxious that
he might miss his train, but in fact half an hour before it was
due to leave. The platform from which it would leave was not
even shown yet on the indicator. Going to the bookstall, he
bought a copy of the *Financial Times* to read on the train, and
it was as he was paying for it that he noticed the woman with
the familiar face watching him.

Not that he could be sure that she was actually watching
him. Their eyes happened to meet for a moment, then she
turned away and walked off along the platform. As soon as she
had done that he could not be sure why he had felt that he
knew her. As usual, when his memory let him down over such
a matter, he felt guilty. Perhaps she had been a student of his

and felt hurt now that he had not recognized her. Or perhaps she was someone whom he knew quite well, who would be thinking that he had been deliberately discourteous. But anyway, she was gone and after all, what did it matter? He strolled back to where he could see the indicator, saw that his train was now shown to be leaving from Platform 5, found that it was waiting there and that he could get into it and passed through the barrier.

Andrew was a tall man and if he took the trouble to stand erect was even taller than he looked, but in the last few years he had allowed himself to get into the habit of stooping. But he had kept his spare figure and still walked with some vigour, though he found that he grew tired now more rapidly than seemed to him reasonable. He had bony features, short grey hair and grey eyes under eyebrows that had remained rather formidably dark. An intelligent face, but in recent years its expression had become more detached than it had been when he was young. His long sight was still good and he needed glasses only for reading. He was fumbling for these so that he could start reading his newspaper after settling himself in an almost empty second-class carriage, because although he could easily have afforded first class, that was one of the minor extravagances to which he had never been able to accustom himself, when he saw the woman with the familiar face looking at him.

She was seated just across the gangway. She was about forty, a slender woman with a thin, pale face with a high-bridged nose, a small pouting mouth and large, slightly prominent dark eyes embedded in a quantity of makeup. Her hair was dark and cut fairly short and she was wearing big, brassy-looking earrings. Her overcoat was scarlet with a collar of black fur. She had a woman's magazine open before her and had been looking over the top of it when Andrew's eyes met hers, but as soon as that happened she looked down, turned a

page and seemed to become engrossed in what she was reading. So at least she did not expect him to speak to her, which
was a relief. But it disturbed him that he was sure he had seen
her before, yet could not imagine where or when he had done
so.

But going on worrying about who she was would do no
good. Opening the *Financial Times,* he settled down to the
puzzle of trying to understand what had been happening recently to his investments. Besides his university pension and
his old-age pension, he had a modest amount of capital, most
of it left to him by Nell, whose family a generation or two ago
had been wealthy and to whom a small amount of their money
had descended. Most of this was in government securities but
a little had been more daringly invested in equities, and although Andrew invariably did what his solicitor told him to
do about buying and selling these, he liked from time to time
to feel that he understood what was happening to them.

Not that he ever really did. But on a train journey that was
too short for starting to read a book, the *Financial Times*
suited him nicely. He had come to the conclusion that perhaps
he was a little richer than he had been when last he had looked
into the matter, when his train, remarkably punctual, stopped
at Braden-on-Thames.

He did not look towards the woman in the scarlet coat as he
got up to leave the train, but out of the corner of his eye he
saw that she had risen too and was making her way towards
the exit at the far end of the carriage, almost as if she did not
want to get off the train too close behind him. He did not see
her on the platform. Yielding up his ticket at the barrier, he
went out of the station into the fine rain that was falling, hailed
a taxi and asked to be driven to Ramsden House, Old Farm
Road.

Presumably there had once been a farm at the end of Old
Farm Road, but there was no vestige of it left now. The street
consisted of fairly large, solid Victorian or Edwardian villas,

all set well back from it in big gardens. Ramsden House was of moderate size, square and covered in cream-coloured stucco. It had a roof of wavy red pantiles and green shutters at the windows. There was a gravelled drive up to a projecting porch in which there was a massive green door with a highly polished brass knocker on it. There was also a bell beside the door. Andrew paid off the taxi, rang the bell and stood waiting.

The door was opened almost immediately by a man in a white jacket and dark trousers. He reached quickly for Andrew's suitcase and let him in out of the rain. This was Laycock, Andrew supposed, the manservant who wasn't quite up to being a butler. Andrew's first impression of him was that he was about twenty-five. He had a round, pink-cheeked, ingenuous face which in spite of its very grave expression was very youthful. He had rather the look of a boy who was doing his best to assume the dignity which he thought appropriate to his occupation. But then Andrew noticed small lines at the corners of his eyes and mouth and after all it seemed probable that he was at least thirty, or even more. Leading Andrew to the door of Felicity's drawing room, he opened it and in a voice more cultured than those to which Andrew in his later years had become accustomed in the younger members of his department, announced, "Professor Basnett."

Felicity was sitting in a chair by the fire, working on some embroidery. She rose with surprising ease for someone of her age, came quickly to meet him and kissed him.

"This is so good of you," she said. "I'm so glad you've come."

She was a small woman who still held herself erect and in whose delicate features and expressive, bright blue eyes it was easy to perceive the beauty that she had once possessed. Indeed, she was still beautiful in the way that a few of the old, in spite of deep wrinkles, sagging skin under their chins and thinning hair can be. Her hair, which had once been softly golden, was now snow-white and was brushed back from her face into a small roll at the back of her head. She was wearing a plain grey dress, a violet-coloured cardigan and a necklace of amethysts.

"Laycock, drinks, please," she said, then led Andrew to a chair by the fire, facing the one in which she had been sitting when he arrived and in which she sat down again. "We'll have a drink straight away, then Laycock can take you up to your room. I don't think you've changed at all since I saw you last. You're wearing very well."

Andrew knew that he had aged a good deal during the last five years, but to the very old woman who was smiling at him with a fair remnant of her once vivid charm, it might seem hardly significant.

"You're doing pretty well yourself, Felicity," he said. "What a nice idea of yours it was to ask me down. It's delightful to see you again."

For the moment, he meant it. Even though he had never been fond of her, he could not help admiring someone who was so indomitably vital.

"You could have come at any time if you'd happened to think of it," she said with some asperity in her voice. Her voice was the oldest part of her. It had once been charming, but now creaked sadly. "But I suppose you're too busy to bother about your aged relations, even though you've retired. I remember you planned to write a book when that happened to you. Have you really done it?"

He thought there was irony in the bright blue eyes, as if she were sure that the book that he had planned to write, about which he must have spoken to her on some occasion that he had forgotten, had never been anything but a daydream.

"I'm working on it now," he said.

The room was very pleasant. It had some good early Victorian furniture in it, some fine Persian rugs on the floor and a number of comfortable chairs covered in flowered cretonne.

There were some hyacinths in pots and two or three quite pleasing seascapes on the walls. Big windows overlooked a lawn with daffodils in bloom along its edges and a forsythia at the bottom. An old-fashioned room without much character, but in which it came naturally to feel at ease.

The door opened and Laycock came in, carrying a tray with a decanter of sherry and three glasses on it. Andrew wondered for whom the third glass was intended until Felicity said, "Laycock, will you please tell Mrs. Cavell we're having drinks now and ask her to join us?"

"Very good, madam," he replied sedately and withdrew.

Felicity chuckled. "Isn't he a dream? I haven't been called 'madam' by anyone else for years. Our daily help always calls me 'dear' or 'love' and Agnes of course calls me 'Felicity,' though I had to tell her to do that when I knew we were going to be friends. Of course, it's three quarters an act with Laycock. He can be quite informal when he chooses. But I don't think he'd like it if I called him 'Ted,' as Agnes does. And really it's so wonderful to have a man about the house. He can pull the corks out of bottles, and unscrew the tops of jars that no one else is strong enough to manage, and hammer nails into things, and change fuses. And of course he drives the car and washes it and does all sorts of odd jobs. He was all my own idea. I saw an advertisement in the *Telegraph* and I rang up about it straight away and got him. Agnes was away on holiday at the time and I had him installed here by the time she got back. I think she rather disapproved at first. Jealousy, perhaps. But he got round her and now she admits I was right to try the experiment."

"How long ago was this?" Andrew asked.

She looked vague. "Three months . . . four . . . I find it so difficult to keep track of time these days. Of course, I don't suppose he'll stay for long. I'm sure he's got his sights set on higher things. Anyway, they never do stay long with you nowadays, do they? It's been so wonderful for me, having Agnes.

She looks after me so kindly and besides that, she's so intelligent. I couldn't stand having an utter fool around me all the time, like that awful woman I had before her. Not that she was exactly a fool . . . No, I don't suppose I ought to say that about her. She was . . . well, other things, and a fool in some ways and of course I had to get rid of her and it seemed wonderful finding Agnes after her . . . Oh, Agnes, come in. This is Professor Basnett."

The door had opened and a small, middle-aged woman had come quietly in. She had a full bosom and broad hips and light brown curly hair, cut short, in which there was still no touch of grey. She had grey eyes, a short, faintly upturned nose and a wide, friendly smile. She was wearing a pale blue hand-knitted jersey and a dark blue tweed skirt. A very ordinary-looking woman, except for the fresh-faced air of serenity about her.

She held out a hand to Andrew and gave his a surprisingly vigorous grip.

"I'm so glad to meet you at last, Professor Basnett," she said. "I've heard so much about you."

Andrew thought it improbable that she really had. It seemed to him unlikely that Felicity had spoken of him from year's end to year's end. Her invitation to him had almost certainly been the result of a sudden impulse. Agnes Cavell, he assumed, merely thought this the courteous way to get over the awkwardness of meeting a stranger of whom in fact she knew next to nothing. She poured out the sherry, then, as she sat down, said to Felicity, "Have you told Professor Basnett our news?"

"News?" Felicity said incredulously. "We never have any news."

"About Quentin," Agnes Cavell said.

"Oh, that." Felicity gave a short laugh. "That won't interest you, Andrew. It's only that my grandson, Quentin, has become engaged. He's brought the girl down to stay with Derek and Frances over Easter and he brought her up here to see me yesterday. Quite a nice girl, I suppose. Not very good-looking, but nice mannered. Not quite right for Quentin, though, I felt. A bit too serious and probably too intelligent."

"I thought she was charming," Agnes Cavell said.

"Yes, yes, of course you'd expect that. Quentin has taste. Have you ever met him, Andrew?"

"Not that I remember," Andrew answered.

"But you've met my son, Derek."

"I rather think he and his wife came to Nell's funeral, but I doubt if I'd recognize them if I saw them again."

"You'll be seeing them tomorrow. I asked them to lunch. Quentin and Georgina are their children. Quentin's twenty-seven. He had an idiotic idea after he left Oxford that he was going to be a writer and he's actually had one or two things published, I believe, but I don't think they brought him in any money, so he dropped the idea and went into advertising, at which I understand he's doing quite well. Georgina can't make up her mind what to do. For a time she thought she'd like to be a nurse, but I think she found it too like hard work, so she started to train as a secretary, but that bored her, so she got a job as courier for a travel agent, but they told her she'd got to take lessons in languages and she said that was expecting too much, so now she's set her sights on becoming an airline stewardess. Meanwhile she lives mostly at home. She's only twenty-three, so I don't suppose it matters much if she goes on fooling around for a time. She knows that when I die she'll have no need to earn her living. This girl Patricia, or Tricia as they call her, whom Quentin's got engaged to, works in his office. I only hope she isn't marrying him for the sake of my money. He's quite capable of having told her that I'm ready to pack it in any day now."

"Now you know that's nonsense, Felicity," Agnes Cavell said. "He's very fond of you."

"But you always think the best of everyone, Agnes," Felicity said. "You don't see what's going on under the surface. Let me tell you, being rich is a wonderful training in distrust."

"Then I'm glad I'm not rich," Agnes said.

"Oh no, you're not! Nobody is. Even the people who renounce wealth and dedicate themselves to total poverty only do it because wealth has such an overpowering attraction for them that they become afraid of it."

Agnes shook her head. "You don't really think that."

"I do wish you wouldn't keep telling me what I think!" Felicity exclaimed with irritation. "You're always doing it, but you don't understand me at all. I'm not in the least nice-minded, like you. As I've told you over and over again, and as Andrew will tell you, I'm not a nice old woman."

Agnes, smiling, looked ready to dispute this, but at that moment the door opened and Laycock appeared to tell them that luncheon was served.

Over lunch Felicity questioned Andrew on how he lived and on who looked after him and was very surprised to hear that he looked after himself, except for help one morning a week when a very competent woman came in to clean his flat for him.

When he told her that he could cook reasonably well and quite enjoyed shopping, she said that she was sure that he had most of his meals at his club; and when he told her that he had never belonged to a club in his life, she shook her head dubiously and said that she did not know what the world was coming to when men could be so independent. When the meal was over she said that as usual she would lie down for a time and suggested that Andrew should do the same. But he had not the desire to do so and, looking out of the window and seeing that the rain had stopped, said that he would go for a walk. Agnes told him that if he turned left outside the gate, the road would take him to a patch of quite attractive common, and that if he continued across this, he would reach the towpath along the side of the river. It was a nice walk, she said.

Setting out about half past two, he intended to follow her instructions and in fact he did so. But first, as he walked down the drive to the gate, an odd thing happened. Someone was at the gate and was just opening it. It was the woman in the scarlet coat whom he had seen in the train. She stood still for a moment when she saw him approaching, then slammed the gate shut and turned away. By the time that he reached it she was twenty yards from it and was walking as fast as she could in the direction of the town.

Andrew rambled across the common and along the towpath, then turned back, taking about an hour and a half for his walk. Although the rain had stopped, it was still blustery and cold and not at all agreeable. The wind had risen since he had started out and moaned among the trees beside the river. But he had felt an urge to get out of the house for a time. He did not know what he would have done with himself, sitting alone in the drawing room while Felicity rested. In fact, by now he was regretting having come. The next few days, he thought, were going to be very boring.

When he returned to the house in Old Farm Road and rang the bell, the door was opened by Agnes Cavell.

"It's Ted's afternoon off," she explained. "He's gone into Braden. I think he's got a girl friend there, though he'd never talk about it. He worries so much about his dignity. Come in and get warm. I'm just getting tea."

She led him into the drawing room where he found Felicity sitting by the fire as she had been when he first arrived, at work on her embroidery.

Tea, which Agnes wheeled into the room on a trolley, consisted of homemade scones, still hot from the oven, little cucumber sandwiches and the kind of fruitcake that Andrew remembered as a normal part of tea when he had been a boy but had not tasted for years. Agnes poured out the tea and stayed chatting until about half past five, when she wheeled the trolley out of the room, closing the door behind her.

"She'll go up to her room now to listen to the five-forty news," Felicity said. "She's got a very nice room with television and her own bathroom on the top floor. She always listens to the news, then she comes down and attends to cooking the dinner. She's a splendid cook. Andrew, you just don't know how lucky I was to find her. I'd been getting quite frightened of getting really old. Derek and Frances kept saying I ought to give up the house and go into one of those very luxurious old people's homes somewhere, but I simply hated the idea. It wasn't that I couldn't afford one of the good ones, but I thought to myself, however comfortable that sort of place is and however much the people there play up to you because you're rich, you won't really be able to call your soul your own. And most of the other inmates will be at least half senile and you'll soon begin to think you're like them. As you may be, of course, without being aware of it. So I took no notice of Derek and Frances and advertised in several papers and I got quite a number of replies, but I picked out Agnes's at once. Her letter was so much more literate than any of the others and I liked her handwriting. A lady, I thought, though perhaps that sounds old-fashioned. And she's promised she'll stay with me for as long as I need her."

"What was she doing before she came here?" Andrew asked.

"She'd recently lost her husband and she said simply that she was lonely and that she'd like a job where she could be of some help to someone. She didn't seem to worry much about the pay. She's got a pension, so the money doesn't mean so very much to her. Her husband was something or other at one of those new universities—Derby, I think. He was some kind of biologist. Perhaps his name means something to you. Eustace Cavell."

Andrew thought about it for a moment, then shook his head. "I don't think I've heard of him."

"I think he was a lecturer, or a reader, or something like that," she said. "He died of a stroke. Very sad, because he wasn't much over fifty. She seems to have been devoted to him. But she really meant what she said about liking to have someone to help. She runs the house marvellously and when I get into one of my moods she only laughs at me, which of course is very good for me. I wish more people had done it when I was younger. I expect they did it behind my back, but never to my face, because there was always that will I was so famous for changing. I'm sure you know I keep changing it every year or so. It's one of the entertainments of old age."

"I hope you've remembered Mrs. Cavell in your most recent one, if she's really all you say," Andrew said.

"Yes, naturally. And I've left you twenty thousand pounds, Andrew. I don't see any harm in telling you about it now. After all, it's why you came to see me, isn't it? So I may as well put you out of your agony."

He stared at her for a moment, hot with anger. Then he laughed.

"I'm glad you warned me of your habit of changing your will," he said. "You can leave me out of the next one, Felicity."

"But why?" Her tone was bland. She was maliciously pretending innocence of having said anything offensive. "It's what I'd have left Nell if she'd been alive and she'd have left it to you."

"She isn't alive."

"No, but it would have come to you if I'd happened to die before her, which really was only to be expected. I'm more than twenty years older than she was. And don't pretend you won't like to have it. You will, you know, when the cheque arrives."

Andrew felt a curious chill. Oddly enough, at the same moment, Felicity gave a sharp little shudder. It was as if a cold breath of air had swept suddenly through the room, touching them both. He thought that Felicity's withered old face turned pale and he began to wonder if she was not as well as she wanted to appear.

"Is something the matter?" he asked.

"Only someone walking over my grave," she answered. "I don't really like to talk about death. After all, it could happen to me tomorrow and I find that harder to face than you might think. Let's talk about something else. Tell me about your trip round the world. Was it very interesting?"

He told her as much about it as he thought would interest her, but he could see that her mind soon wandered and that she hardly listened to what he said. It was after some time, with an abruptness that showed what she had really been thinking about, that she said, "Now tell me why you really came to see me, Andrew. I know it wasn't because of the money. That was me just trying to get under your skin because you never seem to want anything from anybody. It's infuriating to see you so independent and well adjusted."

"I think I came because I felt Nell would have wanted me to," he said.

"You still miss her, do you?"

"And will to the end of my days."

"I missed my husband quite a lot for a year or two after he died," she said, "but on the whole I prefer living alone. I had two or three affairs after his death, but I never felt the least inclination to marry again. It was only when I got old that I began to feel I ought to have someone living with me, and my first attempt at that was so disastrous that I nearly gave in to Derek and Frances and agreed to go into the home they said they'd find for me. But then I found my wonderful Agnes—"

"Just a minute!" Andrew broke in. He jerked forward to the edge of his chair as his memory played the odd trick on him that it occasionally did, all at once revealing something to him that until that moment had been lost in obscurity. "That first attempt you made, the woman you had before Mrs. Cavell . . ."

"Margot Weldon," Felicity said. "The forger."

"The *what?*"

"The forger. She forged my cheques. So of course I had to get rid of her." Felicity had picked up her embroidery again and was stitching at it. "Why?"

"I saw her on the train today, coming down here."

"Did you really? How very odd. Coincidence, I suppose."

"Perhaps. But she got off the train at Braden. Then when I was starting out for my walk this afternoon, she was at the gate. I think she was trying to make up her mind to come in, but seeing me somehow put her off and she went away. I had the feeling when I first saw her at Paddington that I'd seen her before, but I couldn't place her, and it was just your happening to mention her now that made me remember where it had been. It was here about five years ago when I came to visit you and she was working for you. So she forged your cheques, did she?"

Felicity let her embroidery sink into her lap. "Yes. You see, I trusted her completely. It was sheer laziness on my part, not real trust, but I generally behave as if I've no suspicions of people till they make it quite plain I can't go on doing that. I can't stand bothering to be suspicious. It's such a nuisance. But of course my swans quite often turn out to be geese, I'm used to that happening, and I know it's mostly my own fault. But I was particularly stupid about Margot. I let her handle all my housekeeping accounts and cash my cheques at the bank and she knew quite well I hardly ever checked my bank statements as carefully as one should, so actually she got away with hundreds—I'm not sure it wasn't a thousand or two—before I stumbled by chance on what she was doing."

"What did you do about it?" Andrew asked, intrigued.

"Oh, got rid of her, of course. I could hardly keep her on after that. Besides, I'd never liked her particularly. She was a rather brash sort of young woman. I couldn't make a companion of her."

"But didn't you have her charged?"

"Oh dear no, going into court and all would have been too disagreeable. So you saw her at the gate today, did you?"

"Yes."

"That's very strange. I wonder what she could have wanted. she can't have imagined I'd take her on again."

"Have you had any contact with her since she left?"

"None at all. Perhaps she wanted to persuade me she was a reformed character and wanted me to give her a reference. Or perhaps she thought I might give her some money. How did she look? Did she look as if she might be in trouble?"

"I didn't see any sign of it. She was quite well dressed. Would you have given her money if she'd asked for it?"

"Probably, if it wasn't too much and if it was the easiest way of getting rid of her. I suppose she may come back some time this evening. If she came all the way down to Braden to see me and then simply went away instead of coming in, it's rather puzzling."

"Perhaps she lost her nerve when she actually got to the house."

As Andrew said it, the front door bell rang.

"There she is, I do believe!" Felicity exclaimed. "I'm not expecting anyone else."

They heard footsteps, which Andrew supposed were those of Agnes Cavell, crossing the hall and the front door being opened. Then they heard voices, but it was a man to whom Agnes was speaking. Felicity looked interested, but as the talking went on for some time she picked up her work again and went on stitching. It was several minutes before the door of the drawing room was opened and Agnes came in.

"It's really very strange . . ." she began, then seemed unable to go on, but stood looking at Felicity with a peculiar expression on her face.

"For heaven's sake, what is it?" Felicity demanded.

"I think perhaps this gentleman had better come in and explain," Agnes said. She turned and spoke to someone in the hall behind her. "Please come in, Inspector."

A tall man followed her into the room. He was about forty, well built, wide-shouldered, with a square face and a heavy jaw, a short, thick nose and thick dark hair. He was wearing a neat, new-looking raincoat.

"This is Detective Inspector Carsdale," Agnes said, still sounding bewildered. "And this is Mrs. Silvester, Inspector."

"Mrs. Felicity Silvester?" he said, almost as if he doubted it.

"Certainly," she answered.

"I'm very sorry to disturb you, Mrs. Silvester," he said, "but a very unusual thing has happened."

"Yes, yes, well?" she said.

"The body of a woman has been found in the road across the common," he said. "Apparently it was a hit-and-run accident. It looks as if she was killed instantly. We don't know yet how long ago it happened."

"I'm very sorry to hear it," Felicity said, "but what has it to do with me? I haven't been out driving my car. I didn't run over her."

"No, of course not. But does the name Margot Weldon mean anything to you?"

"It does. She worked for me as my housekeeper several years ago. Do you mean this woman who's been killed is Margot Weldon?"

"It seems probable, though there hasn't been any possibility yet of making a positive identification. But her handbag was lying near her and from various cards inside it we're inclined to think that that was her name."

"Was she wearing a scarlet coat with a black collar?" Andrew asked.

"She was," the inspector said.

Felicity gave him a long look as if she were trying to find the answer to some question before she said, "But what's brought you to me? I haven't seen anything of her since she left me."

"It's just that we found a letter in her handbag, signed by her," he said. "It's addressed to the Chief Constable and in it she confessed to the murder of Mrs. Felicity Silvester."

CHAPTER TWO

"Good gracious me!" Felicity said. She stabbed several times with her needle at her embroidery, as if she were punishing it for something. "She said she'd murdered me? How ridiculous. You can see I'm alive."

"Yes, indeed," the inspector said.

"Can I see this letter?" Felicity asked.

"I'm sorry, not at the moment," the inspector answered. "There's a matter of fingerprints, for one thing. But no doubt we'll be able to show it to you later."

"Then tell me what else she said. Was that all, that she'd murdered me? Didn't she give a reason?"

"Yes, in a way she did."

"Then sit down, sit down and tell me about it." Felicity gestured at a chair, then happened to remember Andrew's presence. "This is Professor Basnett, an old friend. You can say what you like in front of him."

Andrew was beginning to think that his visit might not be as boring as he had feared and that the time might soon come when he would find himself wishing that it were.

The inspector sat down.

"There isn't much to tell at present," he said. "She accuses you of having persecuted her ever since she left you, refusing to give her references and maligning her to other possible employers. She describes herself as having been driven desperate."

"You mean she was planning to come here, murder me, post

the letter, then commit suicide?" Felicity said. "Then she was knocked down by a car before she could do any of it?"

"That's the simplest interpretation of what she wrote, in view of the fact that you're unharmed," he replied.

"But there isn't a word of truth in any of it," she said. "She never gave my name as a reference. I've never maligned her to anybody, because there was never any reason to do so. I've had no contact with her at all since she left me."

"Had she any reason to bear you a grudge?" he asked. "Something she might have magnified if she wasn't—well, wasn't quite in her right mind?"

"So that's what you think, is it—that she was insane?" Felicity asked.

"It's a possibility we shall certainly have to consider. It isn't often that a person confesses to a murder that hasn't been committed."

"I thought you were always getting false confessions about things like murder from people who are completely innocent. Exhibitionists. People who long to have notice taken of them."

"Yes, that happens, but it's usually after a crime has been committed and has been well publicized. Not as in the present case, when there's been no crime at all."

"She probably did bear you a very serious grudge, Felicity," Andrew said. He turned to the detective. "Mrs. Silvester and I were talking about it only just before you came. The grudge, reasonably speaking, should be on Mrs. Silvester's side, but if, as you seem to think, the woman may not have been sane, she might have put all the blame for what happened on Mrs. Silvester instead of on herself."

"I suppose that's possible," Felicity said. "You see, Inspector, I sacked her for forging some cheques of mine. I used to give her the cheques to cash at the bank and I wasn't as careful as I should have been, checking my monthly bank statements when they came, and it was some time before I realized that the amount I seemed to be drawing out was about double what it ought to have been. Perhaps I should have called in the police when I found it out. Forgery's a serious crime, isn't it? I believe it was once a hanging matter, though of course that was a long time ago. But I found the idea so unpleasant—I mean the thought of having to give evidence in court and perhaps be responsible for having the silly woman sent to prison and so on—that I just dismissed her. She packed her things and left that very day. And that's the last I've heard of her till today when Professor Basnett told me he'd seen her in the train he came down in himself. And then he saw her again in the afternoon at my gate when he was going out for a walk. He said he thought she looked as if she was trying to make up her mind to come in, but when she saw him, she went away."

"About what time was that, Professor?" Inspector Carsdale asked.

"I think about half past two," Andrew answered. "At the time I couldn't think who she was though I'd a feeling I'd seen her before. It was only when Mrs. Silvester started talking about her a little while ago that I suddenly remembered having seen her here when she was still working for Mrs. Silvester."

"You didn't speak to her?"

"No."

The inspector turned back to Felicity. "You're absolutely sure in your own mind that she was guilty of the forgery? There's no possibility you'd been mistaken so that she might have had a genuine reason for feeling she'd been misjudged by you?"

"Oh dear no," Felicity said. "She admitted it, burst into tears, told me she'd an aged invalid father whom she was trying to support, which I'm certain was a lie, and swore she'd never do anything of the kind again, if I'd only keep her on. Naturally I wasn't going to consider that. I just gave her a month's wages, which I think was generous of me in the circumstances, considering how much she'd got away with already, and told her I expected her to be out of the house by the evening. And that's positively the last I've heard of her."

"How long ago was this?" the inspector asked.

"About five years. I can't tell you the exact date."

He stood up. "Well, I won't intrude on you any longer, but I'll keep you informed of anything we discover. And it's possible we may want a signed statement from you, though I hope we shan't have to trouble you for that. May I say how glad I am that she didn't succeed in carrying out her intention, if she really did come here to commit murder? Perhaps that's what she had in mind when she saw Professor Basnett coming to the gate. If she really had anything in mind. If it wasn't all a fantasy she'd never have dreamt of carrying out in reality."

"But she must have come back later for some reason," Andrew said, "or what was she doing this evening on the road across the common when the motorist hit her?"

"That's something we may never know," the inspector said.

"Was she in the road or on one of the footpaths?" Andrew asked.

"In the road. I expect one of our psychiatrists will come up with a theory about it all, but we may never get any proof of why she came here. If we can trace where she was living, the people there may be able to tell us something about her state of mind, but even that's uncertain. You'd be surprised how blind people can be to the signs of mental disturbance in other people. The symptoms of serious mental illness can get written off as unimportant eccentricities. But, of course, what we're really after at the moment is the man—or perhaps the woman—who killed her. That hit-and-run driver. He's far more of a murderer than she was. But I hope we shan't have to trouble you about it again. Good evening, Mrs. Silvester."

"Good evening, Inspector."

Agnes Cavell let him out.

At the sound of the front door closing after him Felicity sank back in her chair and closed her eyes. All at once she looked as if the detective's visit had been more of a strain than she had allowed to appear at the time. She looked very old and very tired. Andrew turned his gaze to the fire. He had an uneasy feeling that there was something that he ought to have told the inspector and he was irritated with himself because he could not think what it was. For an instant he had grasped it and had been about to speak of it, then either Felicity or Carsdale had interrupted him and now he could not remember what it had been. The probability was, he knew, that if he did not try to think about it, it would come back to him; but it was difficult to dismiss it and until he could it would continue to elude him.

To distract himself he began to recite a verse in his head. Kingsley, of course.

> "Welcome, wild North-easter!
> Shame it is to see
> Odes to every zephyr,
> Ne'er a verse to thee . . ."

The wind outside was rattling the windowpanes. No doubt that was why that particular verse had sprung to his mind. Whether or not the wind was a "North-easter," it had grown even stronger than when he had gone out for his walk in the afternoon. The woman in her red coat must have found it very cold walking in the teeth of the blast out there on the common where there was no shelter. Walking in the road, apparently, to go by what Inspector Carsdale had said, which was odd, or how had she been hit by a car there?

Was that what he had wanted to say to the policeman? Andrew wondered. Had he wanted to point out that it was strange that the woman should have been walking in the road when there was a perfectly good footpath on each side of it? He had walked along one of them during the afternoon. No, that was not it, because of course the police would have thought of that for themselves. It was something else . . .

"Andrew!"

He looked up at Felicity. Her bright blue eyes were open, watching him. He did not know how long she had been doing it, but harmless as his thoughts had been, there was something disconcerting about having been observed when he had not been aware of it.

"Isn't it ridiculous," she said. "I'm frightened."

"In an odd way, so am I," he said, "though I couldn't tell you why."

"Poor woman," she said. "You know, I've a guilty feeling about her now, and I don't like feeling guilty."

"I don't see that you've anything to feel guilty about. Her death had nothing to do with you."

"It's just that if I'd realized when she was here that she wasn't normal—because after all that must be the explanation of the forgery affair, mustn't it?—I might have been a little more compassionate. Though I don't know what I ought to have done, because after all you can't let a person, however mad they are and however sorry for them you feel, get away with forging your cheques. All the same, now that she's dead . . ." She gave a worried shake of her head and an abrupt little shiver.

It was seeing the shiver that reminded Andrew of what the thought had been that he had been trying to recapture.

"Felicity, I've had an odd idea," he said. "Do you remember when we were talking a little while ago before that man arrived, you told me you didn't like talking about death?"

"Well, I don't," she said. "Who does, once they start thinking about it as something that might really happen to them at any time."

"But you gave a shiver and when I asked you if anything was the matter, you said it was someone walking over your grave."

"Well, that's all it was."

"But the odd thing was, I'd felt a chill myself at the same time."

She frowned. "Not telepathy, please, Andrew. Don't let's get ourselves mixed up with telepathy. If you're going to suggest that that's when Margot was killed and that we both felt it because we're psychic, I won't listen to you. It's nonsense."

"It wasn't what I was going to suggest at all," he said. "What I'm suggesting is that we both felt a real draught at that moment."

"A draught?" She stared at him without comprehension. "Where could it have come from?"

"That's what I was going to ask you. Have you ever noticed it before? If a door's opened somewhere—"

Just then the door of the drawing room was opened and Agnes Cavell came in.

"Dinner will be ready in about a quarter of an hour," she said. "Shall I bring in drinks? From the look of you, Felicity, you could do with one."

"Yes, please, Agnes," Felicity said. "And I'll have whisky, not sherry. A strong one. That man's visit upset me." As Agnes went out, she went on, "Well, go ahead, Andrew. What were you going to say?"

"I think I'll let Mrs. Cavell hear it," he said. "She seems a very practical person. She'll be able to tell me whether or not I'm out of my mind."

Felicity gave a little cackle. "And you don't trust me to do that. You're probably right. I've a way of assuming that other people talk nonsense most of the time. And a lot of them do, you know, to someone of my age. Wait till you hear how the children talk to me. So charming, so affectionate, but taking for granted all the time that I don't understand perfectly well why they're troubling to do it, when of course it bores them utterly to come to see me . . . Oh, thank you, Agnes. Yes, whisky was the right thing. Now go ahead, Andrew. Tell Agnes and me what you were thinking about."

He accepted the drink that Agnes gave him and waited till she had sat down with one of her own before he went on.

"It's about that draught that you and I felt," he said. "We both shivered at the same time and we thought it was because we were talking of death and we didn't much like it. But it's struck me since, with the wind blowing as strongly as it is, mightn't we have felt a real chill in here if someone opened a door somewhere?"

"A door from outside, you mean?" Felicity said. "But Agnes opened the door to that detective and then let him out again and I didn't feel anything. Did you?"

"No, but I think that door's on the sheltered side of the house," Andrew said. "Besides, it's in a porch which might shelter this room from any draught there might be when the front door's opened. But isn't there any other door that might have been opened just then and let in a draught that blew through the house?"

"There's the back door out of the kitchen," Agnes said, "and a door into the garden from the dining room. Shall I go and see if you feel anything if I open them?"

"Would you?" Andrew said.

She went out, closing the door behind her.

He and Felicity waited in silence for a moment, Felicity with an uneasy glint in her bright eyes, which she kept on his face.

Then she muttered, "I'm not sure what you're getting at, Andrew, but I don't think I like it."

"It may be nothing," he said. "Just a stupid thought of mine."

A sudden chill swept through the room.

"There it is," Felicity said. "Just the same. What does it mean?"

The feeling of cold disappeared and Agnes returned to the room.

"Did you feel anything?" she asked.

"Quite distinctly," Felicity answered. "Which door was it, Agnes?"

"The back door," Agnes replied. "I didn't bother to open the door in the dining room because the bolts, top and bottom, are shot and no one could have come in that way. Because I suppose that's what you're thinking of, isn't it, Professor? You think that Margot Weldon came to the house this evening, opened the back door and then for some reason went away."

"It's a possibility, isn't it?" he said. "Suppose she'd made up her mind to do the murder she'd got her confession ready for and came here to do it and let herself in . . . By the way, do you normally keep that door locked through the day?"

Agnes shook her head. "I always lock it before I go up to bed, but I don't bother with it while I'm still in and out of the kitchen, because of course I have to go out to the dustbin from time to time and things like that, and anyway, on most days Ted's there. But why did she go away when she'd got as far as writing that confession?"

"Perhaps she came here and heard my voice, talking to Felicity," Andrew said, "and she suddenly realized she wouldn't find her alone, as she'd expected."

"But why should she have expected that?" Felicity asked. "She'd seen you in the afternoon. She'd have known you were staying here."

"That's true—yes," Andrew said. "I should have thought of it. Perhaps it was simply that when it came to the point she realized she couldn't possibly commit a murder. So she went away and walked out on to the common and threw herself under the first car that came along. That would fit with the state of mind she seems to have been in and it would explain how she came to be in the road when the car came instead of on one of the footpaths."

"But I suppose it could have been someone else who opened the door," Agnes said. "Someone who didn't know you were here."

Felicity started up so suddenly in her chair that she spilled some of her whisky.

"Someone else, you say, Agnes!" she exclaimed. "Someone else came here to murder me!"

Agnes looked shocked, as if this were going farther than she had intended.

"No, no," she said hurriedly. "I don't mean that at all. I only meant, someone came to the door who wanted to talk to you privately and heard Professor Basnett's voice and so went away again."

Felicity gave a vigorous shake of her snowy head. "You were thinking of murder. And of course you're thinking now that whoever it was knows a good deal about our ways in this house. He knows, for one thing, that it's Laycock's afternoon off and he knows you've a habit of going upstairs to your room to watch the five-forty news. So he'd have had every reason to think I'd be alone here. Yes, that's what you're thinking. Admit it, Agnes."

To save Agnes the embarrassment of having to answer, Andrew said, "It needn't have been anyone who knows you well, if that's what's worrying you, Felicity. It might have been a stray burglar who'd found out something about your ways, say from chatting to Laycock in a pub, or even from Margot Weldon herself. If she was capable of forgery, she may have had other criminal connections, and if she talked—no, that won't do. She wouldn't have known anything about your present ways here, would she? If she left you five years ago, she wouldn't have known of Mrs. Cavell's habit of listening to the news, or of Thursday being Laycock's afternoon off. So unless she's been in touch with somebody here, she wouldn't have had any information to hand on."

As soon as he had said it, he realized that he had not spoken as tactfully as he might.

"Somebody here—there you go again!" Felicity cried. "It's burglary now, not murder, but you're still trying to involve

one of my friends or relations and to frighten me out of my
wits. I'd never have expected it of either of you."

"I'm so sorry," Agnes said. "I never meant you to take what
I said in that way. If someone really did open the back door,
I'm sure it was just by chance that they hit the time when I
was upstairs and Ted was out. I think the most probable thing
is that it was Margot Weldon."

"I've been wondering where you got hold of her in the first
place," Andrew said. "Where did she come from?"

Felicity gave him one of her long stares, then made an impatient gesture with one of her wrinkled old hands. "As if I could
remember a thing like that after all this time! I know she had
good references. That's to say . . ." She looked confused,
wrinkling her forehead as she tried to think. "No, I'm getting
muddled. It was Laycock who had the good references. I know
about them. I looked into them myself. I don't think I ever
knew anything about Margot's references. Derek found her for
me. But if you think my own son could have been in touch
with her all these years, then informed her about the ways of
the house and suggested to her she should come here and
murder me, you must be as mad as she was. All the same
. . ." With an abrupt movement she finished her whisky and
stood up. "All the same, d'you know, I think I'll just telephone
him and ask him what he knew about her."

She went to the telephone and dialled.

Andrew heard the ringing tone continue for some time before anyone answered. Then he heard it stop and a man's voice
answer.

"Oh, it's you, Quentin," Felicity said. "Is Derek there? . . .
And Frances is out too? . . . I see. Well, I'll leave it till tomorrow then . . . Yes, it is important in a way. A very
strange thing has happened. Do you remember that woman
who used to work for me, Margot Weldon? The one I had to
get rid of because I found she was forging my cheques . . .
You do? Well, she's been down to Braden today and came to

the house in the afternoon, though I didn't see her then, and a policeman's just been in to see me to tell me they'd found her killed by a car on the road across the common, and the extraordinary thing is they found a letter in her handbag, addressed to them, in which she confessed to having murdered me . . . Yes, murdered . . . Yes, of course it's fantastic. The most probable thing seems to be that she was quite mad, but I thought I'd like to talk to Derek about her, because as far as I can remember it was he who found her for me. I don't suppose you can remember anything about that . . . No, I thought not . . . Yes, well, if you like, though I don't know what you can do. I don't even know if I'm going to have to do anything more about it myself. I told the policeman I hadn't seen or heard anything of her for five years, and of course I told him about the forgeries, and I pointed out that I was still alive, so unless I have to identify her or something like that, I don't see what they can want me to do . . . Very well, Quentin, I'll expect you in about half an hour."

She put the telephone down.

"Derek and Frances are out, playing bridge," she said, "but Quentin's coming over. I don't know what he can do, but he seemed interested. We can have dinner before he comes. It's ready, isn't it, Agnes?"

Agnes went out and a few minutes later called them into the dining room.

It was a room very like the drawing room, with good Victorian furniture in it and several seascapes on the walls, which looked as if they had been painted by the same artist who had painted those in the drawing room. Andrew wondered if Felicity had made a collection of his work, or, as seemed more probable, her husband had done so.

There was a good vegetable soup, a casserole of chicken and an excellent trifle, well flavoured with sherry. Felicity asked Andrew if he did not think that she had been very fortunate in finding someone to look after her who, among all her other virtues, was such a good cook. He replied that she certainly was and Agnes laughed and said that she had always enjoyed cooking, but after her husband's death had found it very dreary doing it just for herself. Andrew was helping to clear away the remains of the meal when they heard the front door bell.

"That'll be Quentin," Agnes said to him. "Go and meet him. Felicity will want it."

"But can't I help you here?" he asked. He had taken a liking to the brisk, sturdy woman who had made such a success of her relationship with the often difficult Felicity.

"There's nothing to do," she said. "It'll all go into the dishwasher. Go and meet Quentin. Then perhaps you might tell me what you think of him. I've never quite made up my mind about him."

"Is there something the matter with him?" Andrew asked. "Don't you like him?"

"Oh, I've no reason not to do that," she said. "He's always been very nice to me. But I can't make up my mind how genuine he is. His charm—isn't it silly, but I've always been distrustful of people with charm. That's as unreasonable as taking a dislike to someone because they're ugly."

"So you don't like him."

"No, really I like him quite a lot. It's difficult not to."

"You told Felicity you were sure he was very fond of her. Didn't you mean that?"

"Yes—oh yes, I'm sure he is." She looked put out, as if she regretted the freedom with which she had been talking. "Now do go along and meet him."

Andrew lingered a moment in the kitchen.

"Felicity's very fond of you, isn't she?" he said.

She looked away from him, busying herself with stacking plates in the dishwasher. "In her way I suppose she is," she said. "But I don't know how long it would last if I stopped being useful—you might say almost indispensable—to her. I mean, it isn't me as a person she cares about. And why should it be? I don't expect it. I'm very fortunate to have found a comfortable home here and an employer who appreciates me and who shows it in all kinds of ways. She's very generous to me. There's no reason for me to want anything else."

Yet there was a faint bitterness in her voice, Andrew thought, of which she herself was probably unaware, as if in fact she would have liked something more from Felicity than the old woman gave her. Some warmth that was lacking, some open show of affection.

But he was not inclined to criticize Felicity if she was unable to supply those things. She had been eighty when Agnes Cavell had come to live with her and he had already discovered in himself, at the mere age of seventy, that it became very difficult, as you grew old, to form new relationships of any deep importance. The old relationships—the few friendships that still remained from his childhood and others that dated from his student days and from his early years as a teacher and research worker—had become so much a part of himself that he could not imagine what life would be like without them. But however warm a liking he might take to someone with whom he had become acquainted only recently, it never touched anything deep in him.

He felt an inclination to try to explain this to this woman and to tell her that she should not be hurt if Felicity did not give her anything like the maternal love which perhaps she wanted, but instead he said, "Well, if I really can't help you . . ."

"No, go along," she said.

He went to the drawing room and found Felicity there with a young man and a young woman whom she introduced to him as her grandson, Quentin, and his fiancée, Patricia Neale.

Andrew recognized Quentin's charm at once. It was astonishingly like what Felicity's had once been, a mixture of striking good looks and an unusual vividness and life in his expression. His blue eyes had the same brilliance as hers, and like her he had almost delicate features in a rather pale, pointed face. His hair was the same pale gold as hers had been. He was of medium height, well built but slender, and he was wearing a well-cut dark grey suit, a grey and white striped shirt and a quiet but expensive-looking tie. The young executive, for some reason not quite what Andrew had been expecting.

Patricia Neale was about the same height as Quentin and the same age. She had straight brown hair which she wore hanging loose to her shoulders, brown eyes, a narrow face with a high forehead, a wide mouth and a nose that was not quite straight. She was wearing a dark green dress that hung floppily around her bony slimness and a coral necklace.

"Felicity's just told me what happened here tonight," Quentin said. Andrew noticed that he did not call her "Granny" or "Grandmother." It was unlikely that Felicity had ever allowed him to do so. "There's only one explanation, isn't there? The poor woman was right round the bend. All the same, how lucky it was you were here, Professor. We can't be absolutely certain what would have happened if she'd found Felicity alone."

"It all sounds dreadfully sad," Patricia said. "I'd like to know more about her. Where she's been living. What she's been doing. Do you think the police will tell you anything about her if they find it out?"

"The man said they'd keep us informed of anything they discovered," Felicity said.

"Do you think she was already insane when she was here, working for you?" the girl asked.

"That's something I'd like to talk to Derek about," Felicity answered. "As far as I can remember, he found her for me, and after all, he's a doctor and he rather fancies himself as a psychologist. That's only just struck me. I think it's possible she may have been a patient of his and he thought he could help to straighten her out by getting her the job with me."

"He wouldn't do that," Quentin said. "Not without consulting you."

"Oh, he might have," she retorted. "It's the stupid sort of thing he might really do. He's always so sure he knows what's best for everyone. And he can be a bit of a bully too. I'm sorry to say it of a son of mine, but it's true."

"Would you have given her the job if Dr. Silvester had consulted you?" Patricia asked.

"Certainly not. She was dangerous in her way, wasn't she? All the same, I want to talk to him about the woman. I'm almost certain he recommended her to me and I'm curious about her. It feels so strange, having stirred up murderous impulses in someone . . . You're all coming here to lunch tomorrow, aren't you, Quentin? I can talk to Derek about it then."

Quentin put an arm round her and kissed her. "Yes, of course. Good-night, darling. Professor, please take good care of her. She's precious to us."

Patricia kissed the old woman too. "Anyway, don't brood on it too much. Whatever the explanation of it all is and however tragic it is, it's all over."

"Is it?" Felicity said in an odd voice.

The girl gave her a curious look. "You aren't afraid it isn't, are you?"

Felicity hesitated, then gave her abrupt laugh. "No, of course not. We've had quite enough excitement for one evening. We don't want any more. Good night, children."

They both said good night to her and to Andrew and left.

When they had gone he found himself remembering Agnes Cavell's question. She had wanted Andrew to tell her what he thought of Quentin. But the meeting had been too brief for Andrew to have thought anything at all, except that the young man was unusually good-looking, had pleasant manners and had said nothing that was in any way exceptional. Vaguely Andrew thought that Quentin was not a person to whom he would lend money if he could help it or expect too seriously to keep a promise, but there was no real justification for this, except that he gave the impression of being someone who so far had found the game of living such an easy one to play that he had not had to exert himself much to learn the rules.

Actually Andrew had found the girl the more interesting of the two young people. He liked her slightly crooked yet oddly arresting face and had felt that the strangeness and sadness of Margot Weldon's end had meant more to her than it had to Quentin. But Andrew was never much inclined to trust his own first impressions. They could be affected, he knew, by totally irrational things—a chance resemblance to someone he happened to like or not like, a tone of voice, an attitude to himself that had pleased or displeased him. On the whole, he had liked them both and wished that Felicity was not so strongly disposed to believe that any affection they showed her was for the sake of what she might leave them when she died.

It was at about eleven o'clock that Laycock returned to the house. Agnes was in the kitchen at the time and brought him into the drawing room.

"I thought we ought to tell Ted what's happened, Felicity," she said, "in case the police come back and start bothering us again tomorrow."

"Yes, well, you tell him, Agnes," Felicity said. "I'm too tired. I'm going up to bed. Did you have a nice evening, Laycock?"

"Yes, thank you, madam," he replied formally. "Very agreeable."

"What did you do?"

"We—I mean, I went to the cinema, then had supper in the Ring of Bells."

"And had a drink or two, I expect."

"Well, yes, madam."

"And you went with your girl friend, of course. Why d'you

pretend you haven't got a girl friend, Laycock? We know you have."

"I didn't think you'd be interested," he said gravely.

"Oh, that's the sort of thing that always interests me. Well, good-night. And I think I'd like breakfast in bed tomorrow, Agnes. Bring it up to me about eight o'clock. Good night, Andrew. D'you know, it's a very odd feeling, *not* having been murdered?"

"Good night, Felicity," he replied.

She went out, leaving Laycock looking at Andrew questioningly. There was an odd look of anxiety on his face.

Andrew wished that he could make up his mind about the man's age. He had such a boyish face, yet there were those curious lines on it that should not have come there until he was a good deal older than he appeared. And there was something completely unconvincing about the formality of his manner, almost as if it were something that he had learnt for a part that he was playing. He stood waiting for Andrew or Agnes to tell him what had happened in the house while he had been away.

Agnes made a little gesture to show that she was leaving it to Andrew. He began by asking Laycock if he had heard of Margot Weldon.

"No, sir," Laycock replied. "That's to say, the name seems familiar, but I don't recall where I've heard it."

"She was my predecessor," Agnes said. "She worked for Mrs. Silvester for a short time about five years ago, and she was dismissed because Mr. Silvester found she'd forged some cheques of hers."

"Yes, I remember now," Laycock said. "I think you must have mentioned her to me sometime, Mrs. Cavell. Is that why the police have been here—something to do with the forgery?"

Andrew could not help noticing the apprehension in the man's manner. It worried him, though he reminded himself that at certain social levels there is often a deep fear of the police, together with a conviction that if anyone is going to be suspected of wrongdoing, they will be the first victims.

He went on to tell Laycock, as briefly as he could, what had happened that evening.

The young man stood quite still all the time that Andrew was talking. He had an unusual gift of immobility. He did not even blink, but as his eyes met Andrew's his eyelids were faintly contracted in a way that heightened the look of anxiety on his face.

"Very distressing, sir," he said when Andrew concluded the story.

"Very," Andrew agreed.

"I'm sorry I was absent. I might perhaps have been of some assistance. Actually I was with the lady whom Mrs. Silvester refers to as my girl friend. A Miss Bartlemy. We went to a cinema together where they're showing a film called *The Day of the Red Death*. A horror film and not what would have been my choice normally, but Miss Bartlemy is partial to such things. Then we had a late supper at the Ring of Bells and, as Mrs. Silvester guessed, a drink or two. Then I saw Miss Bartlemy home, then I took a bus home and arrived, as you know, a few minutes ago."

"But nobody's asking you for your alibi, Laycock," Andrew said quietly.

A flush reddened Laycock's pink cheeks.

"No, of course not, sir," he said. "I was just going over in my own mind where I probably was when these unfortunate things were happening. Quite automatic. No sense in it at all. All the same, if there should be any trouble . . ." He paused.

"What kind of trouble do you anticipate?" Andrew asked.

"Well, you never can tell where you are, once you get mixed up with the police, can you? If there should be any doubts, for instance, about the manner of Miss Weldon's death . . . Not that I expect there will be, but if there are . . ." Laycock shrugged his shoulders, as if he were dismissing the matter.

"Would you like your breakfast in your room, sir? Shall I bring it up to you?"

"No, thank you," Andrew said. "I'll come down. What time do you usually have it?"

Agnes answered, "Generally about half past eight, but come down when you feel like it."

"I'll give you a call about eight o'clock, if that will suit you, sir," Laycock said. "Good night. Good night, Mrs. Cavell."

They both said good night and he went out.

When the door had closed behind him Andrew exclaimed, "However did Felicity find him? I'd feel inclined to count the spoons every evening as long as he's here."

Agnes looked disturbed. "Don't you think he's trustworthy?"

"I'm only certain he's never been a manservant before," Andrew answered. "He's acting a part all the time and it's a most unconvincing performance. And the first thing he does when he hears the police have been here is to supply us with his alibi."

She gave a sigh. "Oh dear, I do hope there's nothing the matter with him. Felicity's taken such a fancy to him and she's so pleased at having found him all by herself. I was away on holiday at the time she did it and I wasn't altogether in favour of the idea when I first came back and found him installed. But he's really been so useful and now I think it was a very good thing. And when we're just by ourselves he often forgets about being the perfect servant and becomes quite a normal, friendly young man. I expect today he's nervous of you and trying to impress you."

"All the same, when he heard of Margot Weldon's death, he leapt to the conclusion it might be murder, didn't he?" Andrew said. "Isn't that what he meant by trouble with the police and why he was so quick about producing that alibi?"

She turned her head away from him and gazed down into the dying fire.

"Isn't that what you're afraid of yourself?" she said.

CHAPTER THREE

At eight o'clock the next morning Laycock came into Andrew's room with a tray of early morning tea. Andrew, who had been awake since seven o'clock, his usual time for getting up, looked with a curiosity which he tried to conceal at the young man's face. It had a pleasant smile on it but his eyes did not meet Andrew's. Really, Andrew thought, it was an expressionless face as well as one showing a strange mixture of youthfulness and an almost painful maturity. If he was as young as he appeared at first glance, then he must have gone through a period of suffering that had left deep marks on him, or if he was as old as these marks suggested, then something about him had never grown up.

Andrew had been thinking about him before he had appeared with the tea tray. He wished that he did not feel such distrust of the young man. He found it very uncomfortable to distrust people. Accepting them at their face value was really so very much less demanding than trying to understand what was going on under the surface. In trying to do that he had often made bad mistakes, accepting as a matter of course the honesty and sincerity of people whom he should have seen through at a glance, while he had felt the darkest suspicions of people who were merely diffident and unwilling to expose themselves to him or who happened to be absorbed in affairs of their own which had made them unresponsive to friendly advances.

Yet he could not get out of his mind the oddity of Laycock's behaviour the evening before when he had heard of Margot

Weldon's death. The anxiety that he had shown and the haste
with which he had instantly provided an alibi for himself had
been peculiar, there was no avoiding the fact. And if there was
something dubious about the young man to whom Felicity had
taken such a fancy, it seemed to Andrew that it was up to him
to find it out. For he could not help feeling some responsibility
for Felicity because she was old, because she was not very wise
and because she was Nell's cousin.

She might not thank him for it, because most people prefer
their own illusions to other people's clear-sightedness, but all
the same, for his own peace of mind, he thought, it was necessary for him to do what he could. Not that he had any idea
how to set about it. Felicity had said that she herself had
looked into Laycock's references, so perhaps the first thing to
do was to question her about them.

But she did not come downstairs until nearly twelve o'clock
and by then the other members of the Silvester family—Derek,
Frances, Quentin, his sister Georgina and his fiancée Patricia
—were due to arrive shortly. Andrew had had the morning to
himself. He had gone downstairs at half past eight, absent-
mindedly starting down the stairs in his socks and only when
he was half way down them remembering that in someone
else's house it would be more courteous to wear slippers. So he
had returned to his room, put on slippers and started downstairs again.

At home he was accustomed to a breakfast of coffee, toast
and marmalade and a piece of cheese. At some time something
that he had read on the subject had persuaded him that it was
important to start the day with some protein and naturally to
eat a piece of cheese was far less trouble than boiling himself
an egg. But today, though there had been no cheese, there had
been no need to worry about any lack of protein. Besides coffee
and cornflakes, he had found a generous plateful of bacon and
eggs provided, which he had eaten alone, waited on by Lay-

cock, because Agnes had had her breakfast already and had been busy in the kitchen, working on lunch for the family.

After breakfast Andrew had considered going for a walk, but as he thought of setting off across the common once more, the only alternative to which was to take the road through the suburbs into the town, he had thought that it would mean going past the spot where the body of Margot Weldon had been found. Though he felt a momentary curiosity about it— almost a desire to go and look at the place for himself—he had decided against it and stayed by the fire in the drawing room, reading *The Times.* A little before twelve o'clock Felicity joined him.

She had taken some pains with her appearance. She had discreet makeup on her face, suitable to her age, and was wearing a dress of soft blue-and-grey prettily printed wool. She had a brooch of sapphires and small diamonds at her throat and earrings that matched the brooch. Andrew was not usually observant of such things, but it occurred to him that whenever he had seen Felicity she had generally been wearing some good jewellery. If it was the fact that the sudden draught through the house the evening before had been caused by some would-be thief opening the back door, it seemed not unlikely that he had somehow found out that he would find loot worth his trouble.

"We'll have a drink before the others come," she said as she sat down. "I've told Laycock to bring them. I generally have a drink when I'm expecting the family. I like to be nicely pepped up before they arrive so that they can't sit looking at me, thinking I'm failing . . . Andrew, about what happened last night . . ."

"Yes?" he said.

"Do you think it was really important?"

"Isn't death important?"

"But I mean important to me. Do you really think there's any reason why I should worry about it?"

"I don't know, Felicity."

"Last night I was dreadfully worried. I told you I was scared. That's why I asked Derek to come. And now I feel I've got to find out everything I can about Margot in case—well, in case it was really just the beginning of something. Does that sound absurd? All the same, I think Patricia was probably right and it's all over and there's no reason to make a fuss about it. It's very sad, very distressing, but not really important." She paused, looking at him, then she observed, "I can see you don't agree with me. Why do you think it's important?"

"Only because it's so irrational," Andrew replied, "which perhaps isn't a very rational answer. May I ask you something?"

"Of course."

"You said yesterday you'd looked into Laycock's references yourself. Can you tell me anything about them?"

"Where he's worked before, you mean?"

"Yes."

"It was for a Lady—Lady Something—let me think. I think I've got her number written down in my address book. Do you want me to find it?"

"No, don't bother. You wrote to her, did you?"

"No, we talked on the telephone. She seemed a very nice woman. She told me he'd worked for her for three years and before that had been in the Army for a time. She was only parting with him because she was going to live with a daughter in Canada. She'd the highest opinion of him."

"So she's in Canada now, is she? I don't suppose you've her address."

"Oh no."

"And in fact you'd just the one reference."

"Yes, but it seemed quite adequate. Why, Andrew? What's worrying you about him?"

"It's just the rather odd way he acted after you'd gone to

bed. When we told him about Margot Weldon, he immediately gave us his alibi, just as if we'd accused him of something."

"I'm afraid that's the way some people of his class react the moment there's trouble of any sort," she said. "It can make things quite difficult for one. There's a very nice woman who comes in to clean here every day—not today, because it's Good Friday—and she's been coming to me for years and I've complete faith in her. But one day I mislaid a ring and I asked her if she'd seen it and she blew up in my face and told me that if I suspected her of having taken it she'd give in her notice on the spot. And that would have been an absolute disaster, because Agnes and I are completely dependent on her. And I'd never even thought of suspecting her and of course I found the ring later under my dressing table, where it had rolled when I'd knocked it off without noticing."

The door opened and Laycock came in with a tray of drinks, placed it on a table at Felicity's elbow and withdrew in his dignified way.

When he had gone Andrew said, "I'd feel happier about him if I were more sure about his class. Sometimes, it seems to me, his voice slips into perfectly cultured English."

"That's the result of television," Felicity said. "All the old accents are disappearing. In the old days one could tell what a person's background was the moment they opened their mouth, but you really can't any more. Please pour out the sherry, Andrew, and don't start suspecting poor Laycock of God knows what just because he was a bit touchy about things last night."

Andrew and Felicity had finished their glasses of sherry by the time that Derek Silvester and his family arrived. If it was the drink that had done it Andrew did not know, but Felicity appeared cheerful and animated and a faint flush had appeared on her cheeks which heightened her look of ancient distinction. She and Andrew both had second glasses with their guests.

Andrew found that he recognized Derek and his wife immediately on seeing them, though until he did so he had been unable to recall their faces. Derek, who was about fifty, was a heavy man with a solid paunch and thick jowls and a smooth-skinned, slightly puffy face, with fair hair that was turning grey and already receding from his forehead. He did not resemble his mother in any way. A look of authority gave his otherwise commonplace features a certain impressiveness. Frances, his wife, looked a little younger than he did and was a slim woman with a small face with unmemorable features which had probably been pretty when she was young but had not weathered very well, wispy brown hair and big, worried-looking grey eyes. She was wearing a dark red twin set and matching skirt and a choker of large imitation pearls.

She and Derek went through the routine of kissing Felicity and being introduced to Andrew and saying that they were sure he did not remember them, even though they had been at poor Nell's funeral and had been so fond of her.

Quentin and Patricia lined up behind their elders to kiss Felicity, then shook hands with Andrew. Only Georgina did not join in what was plainly a ritual. She seemed to ignore Felicity, gave Andrew a brief nod, then wandered away to one of the windows and stood looking out at the garden where the trees were bending in the strong wind that was still blowing. She was so like Quentin in appearance that they might have been twins except that she looked a few years the younger, and whereas he was again in his good grey suit and looked quietly well groomed, she was wearing dirty jeans and a dirty, bulgy white sweater. Her shining golden hair hung down almost to her waist. She would have been beautiful if she had cleaned herself up a little.

"Well now, tell me about what happened yesterday," Derek said, sitting down in a chair near Felicity. "Quentin and Patricia told us something about it, but I can't make much sense of it. The woman who used to work for you confessed to murdering you, then got herself run over, is that really what happened?"

At Felicity's request, Andrew was pouring out drinks.

"Yes, and you found her for me, didn't you?" she said. "That's what I want to talk to you about, Derek. Tell me everything you know about her."

"I don't know anything about her," Derek said. "I vaguely remember her working for you and then the blowup when you found she'd forged some cheques of yours, but that's all."

"But you found her for me," Felicity repeated. "You must have known something about her."

"I didn't find her for you," he said. "You must be a bit mixed up, darling."

"I'm sure I'm not. I told you I wasn't going into a home, which was what you and Frances wanted me to do, and that what I wanted was to engage a companion-housekeeper, and you rang me up and told me you'd found just the right person for me. I remember that call of yours distinctly."

He wrinkled his high, shiny brow in bewilderment. "If you're so sure about it, perhaps I did . . . But no, I'm sure I didn't. Really, I'm sure."

"I thought perhaps she was a patient of yours, Derek, and you thought a nice quiet job with me was just what she wanted to cure her neuroses."

"Now, honestly, what do you take me for? As if I'd do a thing like that without consulting you! And she wasn't a patient of mine. That I can say for certain. But I'm beginning to remember . . . Only I'm not sure of it . . . I believe it was Quentin or Georgina who found her." He looked at his son. "Quentin, was it you?"

"No," Quentin said. "I hardly remember her at all."

"Georgina?" Derek said.

She turned at the window and surveyed the room with a faint scowl on her face.

"I can't remember the first thing about her," she said. "I

was still at school when she was working for Felicity, and even if I'd been at home I don't suppose I'd have taken much interest in her domestic arrangements. I can't even remember what the woman looked like."

"But I'm sure one of you recommended her to me and got me to persuade mother to employ her," Derek said. "Cast your minds back. I know it's a long time ago, but there must be something about it you remember."

"It wasn't me," Quentin said.

"It wasn't me," Georgina echoed him.

"Then it was you yourself, Derek," Felicity said, "and you just don't want to admit it. That's just like you."

"Well, I'm not absolutely sure . . . That's to say . . ." He paused, passing a hand across his forehead. "I do remember talking the matter over with you on the telephone, but I couldn't say positively I was recommending her. And if it wasn't Quentin or Georgina who found her, then I don't know . . . Anyway, what does it matter now?"

"Perhaps not much," Felicity said, "except that I feel now one of you is trying to cover something up and I don't like the feeling. But you needn't be afraid I'll hold it against you, whichever of you it is, if only you'll tell me the truth. I'm simply curious, you see. It's a very weird feeling having someone confess to your murder, and I'd like to know more about her. I never got to know much about her while she was working for me. I never liked her much, even before I found she was forging my cheques. But I'm sure you sent her to me, Derek, whatever you say."

"Don't you think it just might have been Max Dunkerley?" Frances said hesitantly.

Who was Max Dunkerley? Andrew wondered. He had never heard the name.

Whoever he was, the suggestion seemed to rouse great anger in Felicity. Her eyes sparkled wrathfully.

"Max? Certainly not!" she said. "If he'd ever done anything

so unusual as to interfere in my private affairs, I shouldn't have forgotten it. Max never interferes. He never gives me advice. That's one of the reasons we've managed to remain friends all these years. No, it was one of you."

If it was, Andrew thought, then of course one of them was lying, and over a matter which only acquired importance because a lie was being told about it. For a moment Andrew wondered if the person who was lying could be Felicity herself. Could she have some devious reason for trying to conceal the fact that she knew more about Margot Weldon than she had admitted?

He had not found an answer to that when the door opened and Laycock appeared.

"Inspector Carsdale is here again, madam," he said to Felicity. "He wishes to speak to you. Shall I show him in?"

Felicity nodded and as Laycock showed the tall detective into the room, she greeted him, "Good morning, Inspector. Can we talk here or do you want to talk to me privately?"

He looked round the room and seemed to hesitate.

She went on, "This is my son, Dr. Silvester, and my daughter-in-law. And these two are my grandchildren and this is my grandson's fiancée, Miss Neale. And Professor Basnett you met last night. And they all know the strange story of what happened yesterday evening. In fact, we've just been discussing it. So I don't think there can be any reason why you can't speak openly in front of them. Because I suppose that's why you've come—to tell me something about that unfortunate woman."

The inspector looked thoughtfully at each face as she named them. It seemed to Andrew that there was something about him today that had not been there the evening before. Something harder, sterner, less inclined to be friendly. His heavy brows had become a straight line across his face.

"We've made certain discoveries about her in which I'm sure you'll be interested," he said. "It wasn't any hit-and-run driver who killed her. She was murdered by manual strangulation and her body was thrown out of a car onto the road. The car was driven over her after she'd been dumped there, but it happens that that failed to disguise the marks on her throat. It probably happened some time between half past five and six o'clock. We've found a witness who was out walking his dog along the road at about half past five and who says he saw nothing unusual then. And it was at about six o'clock that the driver of a van found her and called the police station. And that more or less fits with the medical evidence, though that of course can be misleading. In the circumstances, that letter in her handbag, confessing to your murder, Mrs. Silvester, becomes very interesting."

There was silence in the room.

After a moment, in a dry voice, Felicity observed, "I always thought there was a certain interest in it."

"Of course," the inspector answered without expression. "But what looks probable now is that someone may really have intended to murder you and to put the blame on Margot Weldon. Somehow, probably by threats, he forced her to write that letter. Then he killed her, brought her to the common and threw her body into the road, though he didn't succeed in obliterating the fact that she'd been strangled. And then it was his intention to come here and commit the murder to which she'd confessed, but something prevented him completing his programme."

Again there was silence, then Andrew exclaimed, "The draught!"

Felicity shivered, as if she felt it again.

"So it really was someone walking over my grave," she said.

Andrew explained to Inspector Carsdale what it was that he and Felicity meant by the draught. The inspector thanked him for the information and said that he would hand it on to Chief Superintendent Theobald, who had been put in charge of the case now that it was known to be murder, but it was difficult to discern whether or not he was interested. Coming to what was plainly the main object of his visit, he said that he wanted Felicity to accompany him to the mortuary to identify the dead woman.

Agnes Cavell, who had slipped into the room in the wake of the inspector, protested that Mrs. Silvester should at least have her lunch before setting out. But Felicity said that she would sooner get it over and possibly have lunch after she returned, but that no one should wait for her as it seemed probable that after what must be a far from pleasant experience, she would have no appetite. Derek said that he would go with her to the mortuary. They left in Derek's car, following that of Inspector Carsdale into the town.

Agnes told the others that lunch was ready and acted as hostess, taking the place at the head of the table where Felicity usually sat and giving occasional orders to Laycock, who was more than usually clumsy as he waited on them and on whose cherubic face there was a look of curious grimness. It was as if he was intensely angry about something, Andrew thought. The meal consisted of cold chicken and salad and an apple pie. For a time they were all silent with expressions of wonder on their faces. The first person to break the silence was Frances.

"But it's impossible, isn't it, that someone came here to murder Felicity?" she said. "Who could possibly want to do that? I'm sure that draught was just your imagination, Andrew."

"I hope you're right," he said. "Otherwise I don't like to think about what might happen next."

"That letter in Margot's handbag isn't imagination," Georgina said. "And nor is the fact that Margot was murdered, if we're to believe that policeman.

"And all of us here have perfectly good reasons for murdering Felicity, let alone what outsiders may have," Georgina went on. "The very best of reasons. She's rich and we all need money."

"I don't know what you're talking about," Frances said. "Derek and I don't need money. We're quite comfortably off."

"All the same, we know, don't we, that Felicity's left Father the bulk of her estate?" Georgina said. "And if he had it, he could retire and go to live in some comfortable tax haven and write the book about the psychosomatic aspect of illness that he's always said he'll write some day. I'm not saying, mind you, he came here to murder Felicity. Actually it seems rather unlikely."

"I should hope so!" Frances said.

"But as long as we're talking about possible motives, we ought to bear it in mind that he's got one," Georgina insisted. "So has Quentin."

"Granted," he said. "Felicity's told us she's left you and me each a legacy of several thousand pounds and she's left you her jewellery too. If I had the money now, of course I could get out of advertising and have another go at being a writer. And by the time the legacy ran out I might have learnt the job and be able to keep myself and Tricia in comfort. And that gives Tricia a motive too, because I'm sure she'd far sooner see me writing happily than doing hackwork in an advertising office."

Patricia gave a slight shake of her head. "I'm not sure I would, you know. I like people to recognize their limitations."

"And you don't think I'd ever make it as a writer?" Quentin cast up his eyes in mock horror. "What a shattering blow! I thought you had complete faith in me and my talents."

"I think you've a long way to go before you can be sure about that yourself," she answered. "I think a legacy at the moment might be very bad for you."

"Yet on those terms you think it's a good idea to get married?"

"I'm willing to take the risk. And you aren't going to inherit anything immediately."

Quentin laughed, but the face of the girl, with its oddly attractive, irregular features, was sombre.

"If I had a legacy of several thousand pounds now," Georgina said, "I think I should look for a husband. I'd like to be married, only I don't think I'd like it unless I had some money of my own. I'd hate to be dependent on anyone, always having to ask for money when I wanted some. I know, of course, I could keep on with a job, but I don't see why one should go on working hard if one's managed to get married. Yes, I could do with a legacy."

"Don't, don't, don't!" Frances cried. "I think the way you're talking is horrible. Don't you understand it's perfectly possible someone came here yesterday evening to murder Felicity? To *murder* her! And if Professor Basnett hadn't been here, he might have gone ahead and done it. Why can't you take it seriously?"

Quentin, who was sitting next to her, put an arm round her shoulders.

"It's all right, darling, in our way we're being perfectly serious. We're all slightly in a state of shock, and that's probably why we're letting it out in this deplorable flippancy. But I think what we're doing is quite sensible. We're only doing what the police will be doing soon, and we might as well be ready for them. Who else would stand to benefit if Felicity died? Agnes, what about you?"

Agnes's face, which had been unusually pale, suddenly coloured. "All I know is, she's said she hasn't forgotten me. I've never tried to find out from her what that means."

"It probably means she's done something fairly generous," Quentin said. "I hope so. You've certainly deserved it. Laycock, what about you?" He looked round at Laycock who at that moment happened to be just behind his chair. "Has my grandmother promised to do anything for you?"

For an instant Andrew saw rage in Laycock's eyes. It startled him, it was so violent. Then they became expressionless.

"She has never spoken to me of the matter," he said. "I should not have expected it."

"Then that makes you the most suspicious person here," Quentin said, cheerfully unaware of having aroused any special emotion in the other young man. "It's always the person with no motive whatever who turns out to be the murderer, isn't it? Nothing personal, Laycock."

"Of course not, sir," Laycock said in a tone of icy dignity and left the room.

Georgina had observed more than Quentin. "I'd lay off Laycock, if I were you," she said. "He didn't like that."

"Oh, he knew it was just a joke," Quentin said.

"I don't think he did," she replied. "Or if he did, he was pretty deeply offended. And to tell you the truth, I'd say that even if he hasn't any obvious motive, he might be the most dangerous person in the room. There's something about him that's always given me a queer feeling. What do you think, Agnes? You know him better than any of us. He looked furious just now. Could he be dangerous?"

"Oh, not in the way you mean," Agnes said. "I'm sure he couldn't. I know Quentin offended him just now and I think it was a pity he did it. After all, Laycock could hardly answer back, so it wasn't very fair to him. But it'll blow over quite quickly, I expect."

"I'm sorry, I'm sorry—I know I'm always in the wrong," Quentin said. "If you like, I'll go out and apologize to him straight away."

"I don't think I'd do that," Frances said. "I'd just try not to do it again. Of course, it wouldn't have happened at all if you'd been taking things as seriously as you should. I do wish I could stop you trying to make silly jokes at the moment."

Hoping that he might help to stop any further indiscretions of Quentin's, Andrew said, "Talking of outsiders, people outside this room—apart from the hypothetical burglar whom we mustn't forget, is there anyone you know of who could possibly have wanted to harm Felicity?"

For a moment no one answered, then Frances said hesitantly, "I suppose—well, perhaps one could say Max Dunkerley."

"Max Dunkerley?" Andrew said, remembering that the name had been mentioned once before. "Who is he?"

"He's a very old friend of Felicity's," Quentin said. "He lives by himself in a flat in Braden. He worked for the UN, I believe, till he retired, and he dabbles in painting in an amateur way, and Felicity's told him she's left him all her pictures. All these seascapes she's got. Her husband collected them. They're by a painter called Edwin Hayes who lived around the middle of the last century. I wouldn't say thank you for them myself, but old Max is longing to get his hands on them."

"Are they valuable?" Andrew asked.

"Moderately," Quentin answered. "I happened to notice one of his things went at Sotheby's recently for two thousand pounds. But I think that was a good price. Round about five or six hundred is more usual, I should think."

"So this collection doesn't represent a fortune," Andrew said.

"No. Quite a nice nest egg, but no more than that. But Max wouldn't sell them. He wants them for themselves."

"But he wouldn't do murder to get them," Frances said agitatedly, "so I'm sorry I mentioned him. He's a very nice, very kind old man who's been devoted to Felicity for years. Hasn't he, Agnes?"

"Yes, he comes up to see her at least once a week and I think he's very fond of her," Agnes replied. "Shall we have coffee in the drawing room?"

They returned to the drawing room and presently Laycock brought in the coffee tray.

There was a little silence while he was there, as if everyone felt uneasy at the thought of upsetting him again, and he went

out without speaking. Andrew had begun to wonder if the
doubts with which the man inspired him had been as ill-
founded as he had assumed at first. He had suggested earlier to
Felicity, without himself taking the matter very seriously, that
a burglar with an eye on breaking into her house might have
chatted to Laycock in a pub and found out from him the
habits of its inhabitants. But suppose it had gone further than
that. Suppose Laycock had had a close connection with
Margot Weldon and had arranged with her, without her understanding his intention, that on his afternoon off, when he
had a perfect alibi, she should come to Braden and be seen
close to the house, so that suspicion for the murder that he
intended to commit himself could be easily fastened on her.
That seemed fantastic, because he had no apparent motive for
murdering Felicity. But suppose in truth he had one?

Felicity, as everyone knew, had taken a fancy to him and
might have told him, as she had told Andrew, that he would
be remembered in her will. The amount that she might be
leaving him was perhaps not large by some standards, but to
him it might have been tempting. And suppose he had recently
come to the conclusion that the time had come for laying
hands on his inheritance. Andrew could not believe that Laycock intended to remain a manservant for the rest of his life.
He might have other plans and required a little capital for him
to get started on them.

If that was so, then the murder of Margot, with her confession ready in her handbag, must of course always have been
part of his plot. It was just Andrew's presence that had upset
it. But no . . .

The theory would not stand up for a minute. It was a very
amateurish attempt on his part at detection. For Laycock had
known for several days that Andrew would be in the house
with Felicity. It was someone else, who had not known that
Andrew was coming, who had opened the back door, letting in
the draught that had momentarily chilled him and Felicity,

then had heard Andrew's voice and been frightened off. He wondered if Derek Silvester and his family had been told that he was expected when they had been invited for lunch today. He could not remember that Felicity had mentioned it. It was not something, however, that he could tactfully ask them.

Over coffee in the drawing room there was an attempt for a little while to keep up some kind of conversation, but it soon lapsed. Agnes kept glancing at her watch as if she was wondering when Felicity and Derek would be back from their gruesome errand. Frances said she had a headache and asked Agnes if she had any aspirins and Agnes went out to get them. While she was gone Georgina wandered out too. Quentin picked up a book and started aimlessly leafing through it. Patricia sat quietly gazing into the fire, frowning slightly as if her mind were occupied with puzzling thoughts.

She had a very intelligent face, Andrew thought, and he began to wonder if she was not a little too good for Quentin, who had his own kind of bright intelligence and of course his startling good looks, which no doubt had influenced her, but who seemed to Andrew, now that he had seen a little more of him, superficial and probably coldhearted.

When Agnes returned with the aspirin, she looked round and said, "Where's Georgina?"

"Probably in the kitchen, trying to get off with Laycock," Quentin said. "She can't resist anything male. Of course she'll get a brush off."

"She probably will," Agnes said. "He's fixed up with a girl friend. Oh . . ." She had heard a car outside. "Here they are, I think. I do hope it hasn't been too much for Felicity. I should think she'd better go to bed, then I'll take her up a little lunch and she can rest."

They heard the front door open, then Felicity and Derek came into the room.

Felicity, instead of removing the furs in which she had gone out, huddled them around her as if she still felt the chill of the mortuary and went to her usual chair by the fire and dropped into it. She looked small and shrunken inside her wraps and pale and tired, with the wrinkles that seamed her face deeper than usual.

"Yes, it was Margot—no question about it," she said. "A very unpleasant experience, looking at the poor woman, stiff and stark."

"Have you any brandy, Agnes?" Derek asked. "I think Mother would like it." His smooth, bland face was concerned. "Our outing has been rather much for her."

"I'll get it," Agnes said, "then you must go to bed and I'll bring you up some soup and some toast and you can have a good sleep."

"I don't feel at all like sleeping," Felicity replied. "I feel a rather horrid sort of excitement. But perhaps the brandy will help."

Apparently it did, for when she had drunk it she looked ready to fall asleep in her chair. Her head nodded. Agnes touched her gently on the arm.

"Let's go up now," she said. "I'll help you."

Felicity gave a start as if she had indeed been falling asleep.

"Thank you, I don't need help," she said. "I can manage perfectly well by myself. And I don't want to go to bed. I'll just lie down and rest. Don't bother about any lunch for me. I haven't a trace of an appetite. But bring me up some tea presently, will you, Agnes? D'you know, Derek and I saw the man who's in charge of the case now that it's definitely murder? Chief Superintendent Theobald, I think he's called. Not an impressive person. No presence. I'm sure he won't solve anything."

"I thought he was a very intelligent man," Derek said. "He was so quiet only because he was doing his best not to upset you."

"Why should he bother about that?" She stood up and

walked towards the door. "Nothing upsets me. I'm tough as old boots."

"Darling, are you sure you wouldn't like one of us to help you?" Frances asked.

"Quite sure, quite sure," Felicity answered irritably.

She went out.

It was a moment later, when she had had the time to climb the stairs, that the screams started.

Andrew, who happened to be the nearest to the door, was the first out through it into the hall. The others crowded after him. Laycock, alerted by the noise, came hurrying out of the kitchen and stood staring up with his mouth a little open.

Felicity was standing at the top of the stairs with one arm out, pointing. It was obvious that her shrieks were of rage, not of pain or fear.

"The baggage! The impudent, greedy baggage—look at her!" she shouted.

The door of Felicity's bedroom faced the top of the stairs. It was open and Georgina was in the doorway, looking sheepish. She also looked distinctly ridiculous, for with her dirty jeans and bulgy sweater she was wearing a shining diamond tiara, glittering diamond earrings, a big diamond sunburst at the neck of her sweater and several diamond rings on her not very clean fingers. She looked as if she were not sure whether to start giggling or to burst into tears.

"I didn't mean anything, honestly I didn't," she said. "I just thought I'd like to try them on."

"Whatever did you think you were doing?" Derek asked sternly. "Take those things off at once and apologize to Mother."

"It was just a joke," Georgina said shakily. "I wanted to see what I'd look like in a tiara."

"As no doubt Prince Hal said when he was caught trying on the crown before the King was dead," Quentin observed. " 'Dad, it was just a joke.' "

If only Georgina's head had been visible, Andrew thought, with her pale, silken hair and the diamond crown on it, she would have looked like a fairy princess. It was what was below the level of her neck that wrecked the image.

Felicity still looked furious. "The fact is simply that you couldn't wait till I was decently dead to get my jewellery," she cried. "You knew I'd left it to you in my will, but you couldn't wait to see how you'd look in it. Well, let me tell you, you look a fool. And even if you broke it all up and had it reset, you still wouldn't have the personality to carry off my diamonds. You need something more than you'll ever have to do that. So let me tell you, I'm not going to leave them to you at all. I'm not going to leave you any legacy either." She turned, shrivelled and ancient in her furs, yet curiously frightening in her fierce assertion of dominance. She flung out a pointing finger at the group at the bottom of the stairs. "What do any of you care about me? Why do you come to see me? This silly child's been doing it for the sake of the diamonds she couldn't keep her hands off when she thought I was safely out of the house, but she's no worse than the rest of you. You don't love me, any of you. Not even my son. You love my money and you love the thought that I won't live much longer. You only trouble yourselves about me because you want to make sure I don't change my will. But I'm going to change it. I'm going to telephone my solicitor now and tell him to come to see me tomorrow. And I'm going to leave everything I have, including my jewellery, to the only genuine friend I have, Agnes Cavell. She's the only one I care about and who deserves it."

Gripping the banisters, Felicity came stumping down the stairs.

Andrew heard Agnes Cavell draw her breath in sharply.

"No!" she said. "No!" It was an agonized whisper. "Don't do it—please don't, Felicity. You don't mean it. You know you don't mean it. You're upset by what's happened today. Please don't do it."

"I mean every word of it," Felicity said, turning on Agnes as if she were as angry with her as with the others. "I'm going to phone Arthur Little now and don't think anything any of you can say is going to stop me."

CHAPTER FOUR

There went his twenty thousand, Andrew thought.

Immediately he felt ashamed, but he could not deny the fact that that was the first thing that had flitted through his mind the moment he heard what Felicity said.

The thought that followed it was that perhaps she did not mean to change the legacies that she had left to friends outside her family.

The thought that followed that was simply that he did not need twenty thousand pounds, that he had not thought for a moment until the evening before that he might ever be bequeathed such a sum by anybody and that Felicity had a perfect right to leave her wealth as she saw fit.

By the time he had reached that point, Felicity was at the telephone, talking to her lawyer.

The other Silvesters did not stay long. Georgina disappeared into Felicity's bedroom to take off the diamonds, then joined the family and was shepherded out with them to Derek's car. She was not very popular with them just then, that was evident. Laycock gave a sudden grin which made his round face look boyish, as if the whole incident had been extremely amusing, then disappeared into the kitchen. Agnes and Andrew followed Felicity into the drawing room.

She was just putting down the telephone.

"Arthur's coming tomorrow morning," she said. "Good. I'm glad I've made up my mind about that at last. I've been on the edge of doing it for some time. There was just a sort of unreasonable feeling stopping me that money ought to stay in

the family. But why should it, if they haven't deserved it? And
they don't need it. Derek's a very successful doctor. He can get
on perfectly well without it. And I imagine he can provide for
his own children. And the sight of that awful girl was just too
much for me. Did you ever see anything like it?"

Andrew never had, though he thought that in another ten
years, when she had outgrown the dirty-jeans stage and begun
to take pleasure in elegance, Georgina might be able to wear
diamonds with splendour.

"I don't think you ought to act too quickly," he said, hoping
that it was not of his own prospects that he was thinking. "You
may feel differently tomorrow. As Mrs. Cavell said, you've
had an upsetting day."

"Please, Felicity, *please* don't do it!" The short, sturdy
woman was standing in the middle of the room, her hands
pressed together in a gesture that looked almost anguished.
There was intense anxiety in her grey eyes. "It will only make
trouble. They'll contest the will as a matter of course and try
to prove that I've used undue influence, and I simply couldn't
bear that. Truly I couldn't. And I shouldn't defend the case, I
shouldn't dream of it. So they'd get the money anyway and it
would all be so ugly. I don't mind your leaving me a legacy—I
won't be a hypocrite and say I mind that—but please, please,
don't think of leaving the rest to me. It would make me very
unhappy."

Felicity gave a little chuckle. She looked very pleased with
herself.

"My dear, I've been thinking of doing it for the last year or
two," she said. "I meant what I said—you're the only real
friend I have, so don't argue about it. Now I'll go up and lie
down and presently you can bring me some tea. You haven't
forgotten in the midst of all the excitement, have you, that
Max is coming to dinner? I'd forgotten it myself until just this
moment."

"I don't think you know what you're doing," Agnes said.

"Dear me, you of all people to think I'm not in full command of my faculties!" Felicity said. "Andrew, what do you think? Am I responsible for my actions?"

"Dreadfully responsible," he said, "but perhaps not wise."

"Why not?"

"Because I think Mrs. Cavell's right. Your son would contest your will on the ground of her having brought undue influence to bear on you, and that would put her in a very unpleasant position."

"But anyone who knew me, including you, would be able to testify that nobody, ever, has been able to influence me once I've set my mind on a thing."

"That may be true," he admitted, "but I'm afraid the argument may not make much of an impression on a judge."

"I don't understand you," Felicity said. "Both of you seem to be just trying to stop me doing something I want to do. Something I've a perfect right to do. And I don't mean to let you do it, so you may as well give up. Well, I'll go upstairs now and I'll come down again before Max gets here."

She left the room and they heard her making her way slowly up the stairs.

She reappeared at about half past six. Andrew had been out for a walk, not across the common because he felt squeamish when he thought of it, but into the town, where most of the shops were shut because it was Good Friday and there were not many people about. The wind had dropped and for some of the time that he was out the sun shone brightly in a sky of clearest blue. But clouds had moved up across it before he returned to Ramsden House. It had begun to drizzle by the time that he rang the doorbell.

He expected it to be answered by Laycock, but it was Agnes who opened the door.

"I don't know where Laycock is," she said. "He doesn't seem to be about. I've just taken Felicity's tea up to her. She was sound asleep. You'd like some too, I expect. I'll bring it in a minute."

She wheeled it into the drawing room on the tea trolley almost immediately. There were no scones or cucumber sandwiches today, but there was the same fruitcake that there had been yesterday.

"This is the best fruitcake I've had since I was a boy," Andrew said as she helped him to a slice of it. "In those days we always had a splendid tea, but now it's a meal to which I don't normally treat myself. But I enjoy it immensely when it's provided for me. You're a wonderful cook, Mrs. Cavell. Felicity was incredibly fortunate, finding you."

She gave no sign of being pleased by the compliment. Her face was troubled. At last she said, "You don't think she meant what she said about the money, do you, Professor?"

"I don't know," Andrew replied. "The fact is, I hardly know her. She's only a relation by marriage and I haven't seen her for several years. Is she in the habit of saying things she doesn't mean?"

"Oh yes, often. Sometimes they're quite insulting things and then she makes out afterwards one ought to have known she didn't mean them. And generally I think she really didn't, she was just blowing off steam, because she's been so vigorous and vital all her life and being old now is very frustrating. When she says something particularly unpleasant to me I usually laugh and that seems to make it all right."

"She says unpleasant things even to you, does she?" Andrew said.

"Oh dear, yes. But not things that really hurt. She's never really unkind. But to her family this afternoon . . . She *can't* really have meant it, can she?"

For a moment Andrew had a feeling that Agnes might be trying to make him say that Felicity had indeed meant it and that what she had said could be counted on. But the distress on her plain, snub-nosed face looked real.

"Perhaps when she wakes up she'll have had second thoughts," he said. "Anyway, if she makes a new will tomorrow, she'll probably have plenty of time to change it again. She may live another ten years. Longevity is said to run in the family, isn't it, and I remember vaguely that her mother lived to ninety-six or thereabouts."

"Of course, I know that," Agnes said. "But in the meantime my relations with the rest of the Silvesters aren't going to be very pleasant, are they? Because I'm sure they'll believe I have been using undue influence. It's even making me wonder . . ." She hesitated.

"Yes?" Andrew said.

"It's making me wonder if I ought to give up my job here and look for something else. I don't want to do it at all. I've never dreamt of such a thing until this afternoon. I've thought of this as my home for a long time now. I'm very fond of Felicity and I've made friends in Braden. It would be very painful to leave. But if the Silvesters think I've abused my position in the house, I couldn't bear it. Nobody's ever had any possible reason to think anything of the kind about me before. It makes me feel—well, almost criminal."

"Oh, come, Mrs. Cavell," Andrew said, "that's going rather far. Nobody's going to say anything like that about you. And if they do, you can call on me as a witness to the way things happened this afternoon. It was that silly girl decked out in all those diamonds that upset Felicity. They looked so ridiculous, for one thing, and probably they're very precious to her and she doesn't like seeing them looking absurd. But it surprises me that she keeps them in the house. I don't suppose she wears any of them nowadays, so wouldn't they be safer in the bank?"

"I've tried to persuade her they would be," Agnes replied, "but she says she knows she'd never take them out again once she put them in, so it would be like saying good-bye to them. She keeps them in the top left-hand drawer of her dressing table. She says that's where all women keep their jewellery, that it's the proper place for them. She can be very perverse, you know, when she feels like it. But you don't think it would be best if I left as soon as I decently can? My pay isn't important to me. I've got my pension."

"I think it would be a calamity for Felicity if you left her," Andrew said. "I really shouldn't think of it unless you're unhappy here."

She looked searchingly at his face, making sure that he meant what he said, then gave her wide, pleasant smile and without any further signs of disquiet poured out a second cup of tea for each of them and persuaded Andrew to eat some more fruitcake.

When Felicity came downstairs she looked rested and calm. She said nothing at all about her intention to change her will or her quarrel with her family. She had changed into a long black dress with a string of pearls round her neck. As she had before lunch, she insisted on having a drink before her guest arrived. Agnes brought in the tray with the sherry decanter and glasses on it.

"I don't know what's happened to Ted," she said. She looked harassed and upset. "He's disappeared."

"What do you mean, disappeared?" Felicity said. "Where's he gone to?"

"I don't know. I can't find him."

"Have you looked in his room?"

"Yes, and he isn't there."

"And he said nothing to you about going out?"

"Nothing at all."

"That's odd. He's never done anything like that before."

"No."

"Well, can you manage dinner without him?"

"Oh, I can manage all right. It's just that it's strange."

"When d'you think he vanished?"

"I don't know. He didn't seem to be around this afternoon. I had to open the door to let Professor Basnett in, but I thought perhaps Ted was just upstairs, watching television, and hadn't heard the bell. He often does that in the afternoon. But he isn't there."

"Well, let's not bother about him now," Felicity said. "Max will be here any time now and Laycock may just walk in. You don't suppose . . ." She stopped.

"Yes?" Andrew said. Agnes had left the room.

"I was just going to say, you don't suppose the police have taken him in for questioning about that affair yesterday? I don't know why they should, but suppose they have. Only I think he'd have let us know they were taking him away, don't you? It's a little worrying. But I don't want to let myself get worried and upset when I'm expecting Max. He's such a dear man. I know you'll like him."

It was about seven o'clock when Max Dunkerley arrived. At first sight Andrew did not feel at all sure that he was going to like him. He was a short, portly man of about sixty-five with a large, fleshy face, wide-open blue eyes with a look in them of almost continuous surprise, and only a little hair left, which was long enough to curl over his collar. It was nearly white, but had a faint, pinkish tinge in it, as if it had once been red. He had large feet which pointed slightly outwards as he tramped forwards into the room and kissed Felicity.

"Now what's all this I've been reading about in my evening paper?" he asked when she had introduced Andrew. "About a murder on the common. Probably you don't take an evening paper, but have you heard about it?"

His voice was high-pitched and grating and sounded as if it belonged to a much older man than he appeared to be.

"Have we *heard* about it!" Felicity exclaimed. "It's our own special murder. D'you mean there was nothing about us in the paper?"

"Not a word, my dear. Why should there be?"

"Well, it's true we haven't had any reporters round," she

said. "I hadn't thought of that. So the police are keeping quiet about that side of it, are they? I wonder why."

He sat down. "Mind if I smoke?" He did not wait for permission to light a cigarette with his short, thick, nicotine-stained fingers. "Now go on, go on, tell me how you're mixed up in it."

"But didn't it even mention in your evening paper that Margot Weldon used to work for me?" Felicity asked.

"So that's who the woman was. The name seemed familiar, yet I couldn't place it. No, they only said that the body of a woman who had been identified as a Miss Margot Weldon, of some address in London, I forget where it was, had been found yesterday evening on the road across the common out here, probably strangled and dumped from a car. That's all."

"So they know her address. I suppose it was in her handbag, along with that peculiar letter of hers. Andrew, please tell Max about the letter."

Andrew did his best to give a short account of Margot Weldon's strange confession and of her visit to the house in the afternoon before her death. He was not going to mention the odd circumstance of the draught that had blown through the house, which both he and Felicity had felt, but she prompted him to do it. Max listened with his staring eyes fastened unblinkingly on Andrew's face. He looked deeply interested, and when Andrew finished, he nodded his head several times.

"It's all as clear as day, isn't it?" he said. "It's just as your policeman said. Someone somehow forced the woman to write the letter, then murdered her, drove out here, dumped her body, drove his car over it to make it look like an accident, came on here to murder you, Felicity darling, assuming the confession in the handbag would keep him in the clear, but then he had all his plans upset because when he let himself in at the back door, he heard Professor Basnett's voice in here, talking to you. Whoever it was, was a sad bungler, wasn't he? Not to have made a better job of driving his car over the woman's body so that the strangulation really was hidden, and not to be completely certain you'd be alone. Why, I might have been here myself when he came. Don't I often drop in for a drink with you about that time? Of course, you suspect some member of your family. That's understandable. What we must make sure of is that he isn't successful when he has another go."

"Max, how *can* you?" Felicity cried. "What terrible things you're saying! Oh, why in the world do I put up with you?"

"Because you like having your own thoughts put into words," he said. "Professor Basnett has a kind face. I'm sure he'd do his best, but he'd never be able to plumb the terrible depths of your mind. There's a great deal of buried evil in your mind, so it doesn't really startle you that there may be evil in your nearest and dearest. Now the question is, what are we going to do about it? Would you like to come and stay with me?"

"In that unspeakable little flat of yours? No, thank you, Max." She laughed. "You mean well, but I couldn't stand it. And as it happens, I've made arrangements to protect myself. Arthur Little is coming out here tomorrow to draw up a new will for me in which I'm leaving everything I've got to Agnes. So none of the family will have any motive for murdering me. And they know that already. I told them what I was going to do this afternoon. So if I get murdered before Arthur gets here, whoever does it had better not bungle his alibi as he's bungled things so far, because his motive will be rather obvious."

So that was her real reason for changing her will, Andrew thought. He ought to have understood it sooner. It was perhaps a better reason than the one she had given before.

Max Dunkerley let cigarette ash drift on to his waistcoat. "Then come and stay with me tonight," he said. "You can have my bedroom and I'll sleep in the studio. I've often done it before and it's quite comfortable, though I'd sleep on the floor if I thought it was for your good, Felicity." He sounded troubled and sincere and Andrew began to like him better than he had until then. "It need only be until you've got things sorted out with Little. Just the one night."

"My dear, you really are very kind," she said, "but I'll have two strong men to look after me here in the house tonight, Andrew and Laycock. And I never sleep a wink in a strange bed and I feel terrible if I don't sleep. So I'll just risk it and stay at home."

He gave a little shake of his head, as if he did not like the sound of it, but knew only too well that arguing with Felicity was generally fruitless. A few minutes later Agnes came into the room to tell them that dinner was ready.

It looked as if Felicity had been mistaken when she said that there would be two strong men in the house that night, for there was still no sign of Laycock. Agnes was deeply agitated by his mysterious absence and could not stop talking about it, which Andrew saw irritated Felicity. She was worried too, but her way of dealing with it was to brush it off as something that it was better not to think about.

"If he doesn't turn up soon with a very good explanation of what he's been doing, of course I shall dismiss him," she said as they sat down at the table in the dining room. "I don't understand it. It doesn't seem like him. He's always seemed so considerate and responsible. So he may have some good reason for what he's done, though I can't imagine what it could be. If he's gone off simply because he's had some trouble with that girl friend of his or something of that sort, I shall have to get rid of him. If he thinks we've become so dependent on him that he can do what he likes, I really can't tolerate it. Oh dear, what a pity! We seem to have had our domestic affairs so comfortably arranged for a good while now, haven't we, Agnes? And the silly boy has to go and upset things. How I do wish people had more thought for others. But times have changed. People aren't nearly as reliable as they used to be."

Andrew did not believe that Felicity had ever had much thought for others. Her own comfort had always been the main object of her life. But the disappearance of Laycock was certainly strange.

"Have you looked in his bedroom to see if he's taken anything with him?" he asked Agnes. "It might tell you whether or not he means to return."

"Goodness me, you don't mean to say you think he may have gone off for good!" Felicity exclaimed.

"It's a possibility, isn't it?" Andrew said.

"Suddenly, without a word of warning?"

"People do that sort of thing sometimes," he said. "For no reason that anyone can understand, they just disappear. Have you looked in his room, Mrs. Cavell?"

"Only quickly, to see if he was there," she said. "But I shouldn't know it if he'd taken anything with him. I don't know anything about his belongings. He's always looked after his room himself."

"I expect he'll turn up presently with some perfectly good explanation of what's happened," Max Dunkerley said, sounding as if he meant it to be encouraging, but there was such a lack of confidence in his tone that it could not have had that effect.

Certainly it did not succeed in cheering Agnes. A brooding look remained on her face and she hardly spoke for the rest of the meal. Max also became unexpectedly silent. Andrew had a feeling that he was a naturally garrulous man who in normal circumstances might prevent any real conversation from getting under way simply by drowning it in his own chatter. But not tonight. He was abstracted and spoke only briefly when he was spoken to. On the whole it was not a successful evening, and Felicity, realizing that it was not, showed her annoyance and swept out of the room as soon as she could, taking Agnes with her, leaving the two men together.

They were both silent for some time, then Andrew, feeling

that he must say something, inquired, "Have you known Felicity a long time?"

"Oh yes, I met her soon after she came to live here," Max answered. "That must be nearly twenty years ago. I knew Derek and Frances already and the two children, so I met Felicity and fell in love with her. I mean that almost literally. If she'd been ten years younger I'd have asked her to marry me. She'd only have been ten years older than I and what's ten years when you fall passionately in love? I can't tell you how beautiful she was, even in her sixties. Not that she'd have accepted me. She doesn't really like anyone to come too close to her. I believe Agnes has been about the best friend she's ever had, and she, of course, has to remember her position and do what she's told. She doesn't seem to mind it, but that sort of relationship wouldn't have suited me. We should have been extremely unhappy. Ah well." He gave a sigh. "Perhaps things are best as they are. She really is going to make a new will, leaving everything to Agnes, is she?"

"So I believe."

"It seems to me sad, somehow. I'm quite fond of the whole family, even that rather dreadful girl Georgina. She'll be all right when she grows up. I know she's taking her time about it, but I've known her since she was a toddler and she was so sweet then. I suppose that's given me a special sort of feeling about her. And I like this girl Quentin's got engaged to. He's showing better sense than I expected. And Derek's a very good sort of fellow. An excellent doctor, conscientious and understanding. And Frances may be a bit of a muddler, but I've never known her do anything unkind."

"So after all you don't really believe anyone in the family tried to get in and murder Felicity?"

"Good heavens, no! That's what *she* thinks, that's all. I haven't the faintest idea who did it, unless it was that man Laycock. That seems as probable as anything. But I don't go in for solving murder mysteries. Shall we join the ladies?"

He stood up.

However, when Andrew went to the drawing room, Max disappeared into the lavatory, so Andrew entered the room alone.

Felicity at once addressed him rapidly, in a low tone, as if she were afraid that Max might overhear her. "Andrew, tell me quickly, did Max say anything about the pictures?"

"No," he said.

"You see, it's obvious he was depressed at dinner and I've been wondering, when I told him I was going to leave everything to Agnes, did he think I meant the pictures too? Because he's longing to have them and I promised them to him years ago. Of course I couldn't change that."

"Do they mean a lot to you?" Andrew asked. "Are you very fond of them?"

"Not specially. As a matter of fact, I've never cared for them much. Seascapes don't mean anything to me. It was James who collected them."

"Then why not make Dunkerley a present of them right away? That would relieve his anxiety."

"A present? Right away?" The idea seemed to astonish her and on the whole to displease her. Once she had parted with them, Andrew realized, she would feel that she had lost at least some of her power over Max Dunkerley. With an odd pang of pity, Andrew thought suddenly what a very lonely person she must be, believing, as she did, that no one could care for her except for the sake of her possessions.

"I'll think about it," she said. "Perhaps it would be the best thing to do. But there'd be the blank spaces on the walls. The wallpaper's probably faded. I'd have to have the rooms redecorated."

When Max joined them a minute or two later, she said nothing about the pictures and they had not been mentioned when, at half past ten, he left the house.

Felicity said good-night to Andrew and Agnes and went up

to bed almost at once. Andrew asked Agnes if he could help
her clear the table in the dining room, but with a weary yawn
she sank into a chair, replying that she was very tired and
would leave it till next morning. She could easily do it before
she got the breakfast, she said. She looked worn out. Her face
was drawn and her eyes, which were usually so calm, had an
anxious, concentrated look in them, as if she were dwelling
intently on something in her own mind. She and Andrew sat
quietly for a little while and Andrew was just about to say
good-night and leave her when they heard Felicity calling.

"Agnes! Agnes, will you please come up here?"

She gave a little groan, as if the effort were almost too much
for her, then pulled herself to her feet and went out.

Andrew remained where he was, half expecting the sounds
of a rumpus to start upstairs. Felicity's voice had sounded
excited. But all was quiet and incautiously he allowed his eyes
to close. That was all that he intended at the moment, just to
let them close briefly. Then he would go upstairs and go to
bed.

What a pity it was, he thought, that it would not be his own
bed in his own room. Although Felicity's spare bedroom was a
good deal more luxurious than his own, it did not seem to him
to be nearly so restful. It was merely the unfamiliarity of it, of
course, that gave him that feeling. The bed could not have
been more comfortable. There was a bathroom opening out of
it. There was a bookshelf with a promising-looking collection
of books for the wakeful guest. But all the same, how peaceful
it would be to be at home now, without thoughts of murder to
trouble him, or policemen coming and going, or wills that
needed changing . . .

"Professor Basnett! Professor Basnett!"

He woke with a start. Agnes had a hand on his shoulder and
was shaking him. He had no idea how long he had been asleep.

"I'm so sorry," he mumbled drowsily. "I must have
dropped off."

"I'm sorry to disturb you," she said, "but there's something I'd like to show you. Something very odd. I'd like to know what you think of it."

He felt too sleepy to be able to think clearly about anything, but he stood up and followed her out to the kitchen.

The back door was standing wide open.

Doing his best to dismiss the fog of fatigue from his mind, he said, "Did you open it?"

"Of course not," she answered. "I came in here just now to lock it and found it like that. And it must have happened since I was in here, making the coffee. I haven't been back since I did that, but the door was shut then."

"So someone came in after that," Andrew said, "and left in a hurry, or why didn't he shut the door behind him? Do you suppose it was Laycock?"

For some reason the question seemed to anger her.

"Laycock, Laycock!" she cried. "Can't anyone think of anything but Laycock? Anyway, why should he leave the door wide open like that if he came home?"

"Suppose he was drunk and didn't know what he was doing?" Andrew said. "D'you think there's any possibility he's an alcoholic?"

"I'm certain he isn't," she snapped at him. "He hardly ever drinks anything."

"But suppose he's been one in the past and just had a lapse today." Andrew felt fairly sure he was talking nonsense, but he could not think of anything else to say. "Suppose he found the murder and the police and so on a bit too much for him and wandered off, looking for consolation. Then he might have come back, very drunk, a little while ago and gone up to bed. Have you looked in his room?"

"No, but I will. I certainly will. I'm positive you're wrong."

She still seemed angry at the suggestion. Closing the door, she locked it and shot the bolts at top and bottom, then ran to the foot of the staircase.

All at once her aggressiveness drained out of her. "Of course, you may be right," she said in a troubled voice. "It would explain quite a lot of things. Why he's doing the kind of job he is, when he's obviously too good for it . . ."

With dragging feet, she went slowly up the stairs.

In a few minutes she came down again.

"No," she said, "he isn't there. There's no sign he's been there since the morning. The room's perfectly tidy. He's always very tidy. It must have been someone else who opened the door."

"Or the latch didn't quite catch the last time you shut it," Andrew said, "and the wind's blown it open."

"Only there's no wind tonight."

It was true. The night was still and even while the door had been open there had been no feeling of a cold blast blowing in. In a clear sky stars had been shining brightly.

"You don't think . . ." Agnes began uncertainly and paused. "You don't think that—just possibly—whoever came in may still be in the house?"

In fact the thought had occurred to Andrew, but he had not wanted to alarm her by telling her of it, though he felt that before going to bed it would be his duty to look through the house. Felt it reluctantly, because he had not the least desire to come face to face with a probably violent intruder. However, as she had brought the matter up herself, he decided to admit what had been in his mind.

"It isn't impossible," he said.

"Then oughtn't we to look round?"

"Yes—yes, no doubt." He went back to the drawing room and picked up the poker. Agnes followed him. "If you'll wait here I'll go round—"

"Oh, I'll come with you," she said. "It'll be better if there are two of us. And we must be very quiet. We don't want to disturb Felicity."

They set off through the house.

In only a few minutes Andrew decided that it should be Agnes and not he who was carrying the poker. She hurried from room to room ahead of him, looked inside cupboards and under beds with a boldness which made him feel how pusillanimous he was himself. She went ahead with intrepid haste while he was inclined to go slowly, with a good deal of caution.

In Laycock's room on the top floor she made a particularly careful examination of cupboards and drawers and of the small bathroom opening out of the bedroom. Apart from establishing the fact that neither he nor anyone else could be hiding there, she appeared to be looking for something special. When she failed to find it, she stood still in the middle of the very tidy room, looking round with an air of disappointment.

"I thought—I just had a sort of idea—that his suitcase might be here and that if it was, it might tell us something," she said. "Of course I was away when he arrived, so I don't know for sure how much luggage he brought, but I know he had a suitcase, because I've seen it on top of that cupboard." She pointed. "But it's gone. So I suppose he's left and isn't coming back. Yet he's left quite a lot of things—shirts and socks and so on—in his drawers. So I don't know what to make of it. Let's get on."

She led the way into her own bedroom which was on the same floor, found it as empty as the other rooms in the house, then led the way downstairs again.

Back in the drawing room she suggested that Andrew might like a nightcap and admitted that for once she felt inclined to have one herself. She brought in whisky and glasses and left Andrew to pour out drinks for them. The energy that had carried her through their search of the house seemed suddenly to have run out. A look of depression had settled on her features. She began by gulping her drink, as if she could not wait to feel the warmth of it inside her, then, catching herself doing this, put the glass down on a table at her side, gave a slight shudder and sat back, closing her eyes.

Andrew sipped his own drink slowly, watching her for a little while and wondering whether to call her back from the distance to which she had withdrawn or to leave her to come back in her own time. In the end he cleared his throat to remind her that he was there and asked a question that had been on his mind for some time.

"Mrs. Cavell, do you remember when Felicity called you upstairs soon after she went up to bed?"

She started and opened her eyes. "Yes?"

"It isn't a question I've any right to ask," he said, "but she sounded excited. Was it about anything special?"

She reached out a languid hand to pick up her glass again, but then nursed it without drinking.

"Yes, it was special in a way," she said, "and she'd worked herself up into quite a state of excitement about it. It was about the money. As a matter of fact, it rather upset me."

"You mean she told you she hadn't meant what she said about changing her will?"

"No, she told me she *had* meant it."

"She told you she was definitely going to leave all her money to you?"

"Yes. She'd realized, you see, that I hadn't believed it, so she called me upstairs so that we could have a quiet talk and told me very emphatically that she'd meant every word she'd said because I was her only real friend and that when Mr. Little came tomorrow she would make a will which would convince me she was serious. And so she really is at the moment, I think, but of course she'll have plenty of time to change her mind again. She may live to a hundred."

"And it upset you that she's going to leave her money to you?"

"Yes, it did, it upset me."

"But why?"

"For the reasons I gave her this afternoon. The family would contest the will on the grounds that I'd used my position here to gain undue influence over her, and I couldn't bear to put up a fight about a thing like that. Of course I'd like to have the money. Don't imagine I wouldn't. But not at the price of having a horrible action in court and being made to appear a greedy, grasping woman who'd done all she could to get her hands on a fortune. I've really never done anything of that kind, you know."

"I'm sure you haven't."

"Felicity told me some time ago that she'd left me a legacy, and I'm very glad she wanted to do that and I'd have no hesitation at all about accepting it, and I don't think her family would grudge it me. But all her money, no—no, it simply wouldn't do."

"A good many people would gamble on their chances of being able to hold on to it," Andrew said, "even if it meant fighting an action in court."

"Oh, I know, and don't think for a moment I'm not tempted. Even though I've never been really poor in my life, I've never been rich either, and there are so many things one might do . . ." She gave a long, quiet sigh. "Yes, of course I'm tempted. But I understand myself enough to know I'd give in, and then I'd be hurt and disappointed and upset much more than if I give up all hope of it now. And even if I didn't give in and if I won the case, I'd have the feeling there was something horribly sordid about it. Dishonest, almost. It's a feeling that goes very deep in most of us, doesn't it, that money should stay in the family?"

"I suppose so, though I don't see why it should if they don't deserve it." Years ago Andrew had made a will leaving his own modest estate to a nephew who was almost his only living relative and of whom he happened to be very fond, so there had been no problem for him. "But you won't want to go on working for ever, you know. The time will come when you

might be very glad to have Felicity's money behind you, even
if it turns out to be rather less that it sounds now, because I
suppose Inland Revenue would take a good slice of it."

"I shan't need it," she said. "My husband was a reader in
molecular biology at the University of Derby, so I've got my
share of his pension. It's not very much, but it's enough to get
by on. I don't really need to work, I just wanted to. I felt so
lonely after his death, and I found it so boring cooking just for
myself and so on that I decided I'd try to get a job where at
least I'd be of use to someone. And I just happened to land
here. Of course, Felicity can be very trying sometimes and
quite often I say to myself I simply won't stand it any longer
and I'm going to leave and look for a job with people who
won't be so demanding. Because she does demand a lot, you
know, in the way of attention and giving in to her whims. But
the fact is, I'm very fond of her and I think she is of me, after
her fashion. So I just stay on."

"What d'you really think about the way Laycock left this
afternoon?" Andrew asked. "Why d'you think he did it?"

She looked deeply into her glass, giving herself a moment to
think. Then she shook her head.

"I simply don't know."

"Do you trust him?"

"Don't you?"

"No, I don't. Even before he disappeared I had my doubts
about him."

"He's always been very helpful and efficient." She sounded
defensive, as if even now she was unwilling to criticize the
young man. "I've always liked him."

"But his performance as a manservant wasn't very convinc-
ing, was it?"

"Wasn't it? I don't know what a manservant ought to be
like. I don't think I've ever met one before."

"I'm not sure that I have either, but I couldn't help feeling
he'd learnt his behaviour from rather old-fashioned West End

comedies. I suppose he wasn't ever an actor who couldn't make it in the theatre and found that a job like this one with Felicity felt nice and secure?"

"But he worked for someone else before he came here—worked for her for three years, I believe."

"Ah yes, I was forgetting that. Well, perhaps he'll just come back tomorrow with or without an explanation of what he's been doing." He saw a little animation come back into her expression and wondered if Laycock, with his boy's face, had succeeded in appealing to a frustrated motherliness in her. "You've no children?" he asked. "There's no one to look after you?"

"No," she answered. "Anyway, if I had any, I shouldn't want them to do that."

"And you've never thought of marrying again?"

She gave an unexpectedly gay little laugh. "D'you know, it's funny your saying that, because I had a proposal only a few weeks ago. Yes, at my age! It was from Max Dunkerley. Can you imagine that?"

"I can't really see why not," Andrew answered. "But I gather you weren't interested."

"I'm afraid not—no. I like him, you know. He's been a good, loyal friend to Felicity and he's always been very nice to me, but as a husband, well . . ." She gave another laugh. But then the cheerfulness faded from her face. "I loved my husband very much, you see. We got married when we were very young and I don't think either of us gave a thought to anyone else ever after. It was so wonderful while it lasted. At first, when he died, I simply couldn't believe it had happened. Life couldn't be like that, I thought. I don't think I could ever think of replacing him, even by someone I was fond of."

Andrew thought of what a power for loving was going to waste in this woman and of how much waste of this kind there was in a world that seemed sometimes to be given over almost wholly to hatred and destruction. But his own case, after all, was not so different from hers and he knew there was nothing to be done to bring that old power, once lost, back into use.

Tears had suddenly come into her eyes. She knew that he had seen them and did not try to hide them.

"Forgive me, I'm not often like this," she said. "But it's a long time since I've had someone like you to talk to. And it's been a trying day. I'm not myself."

She finished her drink and stood up.

"Good night," she said.

Andrew stood up too. "Good night."

She paused to put the fire screen in front of the remains of the fire, then asked him to remember to turn out the lights when he went up to bed and left him.

He did not linger for long in the drawing room after she had gone, though he thought that he was too restless and wide-awake to have any chance of sleeping. But in his bedroom he found an Agatha Christie which he did not think he had read, so he got into bed, switched on the table lamp beside it and settled down to read.

However, he must have been more tired than he realized, for almost at once the print began to swim before his eyes, he could not keep his mind on the characters who were being introduced at the beginning of the story, and after only a little while he discovered with a start that the book was flat on his chest and that undoubtedly he had been asleep for at least a few minutes. Laying the book down, he switched off the light and was soon in a deep sleep.

He woke, as he usually did, at about seven o'clock. Yesterday, he remembered, Laycock had brought him tea at eight o'clock, but this morning, presumably, there would be no Laycock and so no tea, unless the young man had returned during the night, with or without an explanation of his absence. But in any case, eight o'clock seemed a long way off and Andrew found that he had intense desire for a piece of cheese.

He was of course accustomed to starting his day with a

piece of cheese, but he had not recognized till then that this had become virtually an addiction. He knew that Agnes Cavell would presently provide him with a substantial breakfast in which there would be no lack of protein, but all the same, what he wanted as he lay there, watching through the window the April sky become sunny and softly blue with no trace of cloud in it, was a piece of cheese.

For a little while he controlled himself, but at last, thinking that for sure he would be able to find some in the kitchen, he got up, put on his dressing gown and a pair of socks and crept quietly downstairs.

As soon as he approached the kitchen he realized that he was not the first person astir in the house. Agnes was there already, busy with the clearing up of the meal that had been left in the dining room the evening before. He thought that she looked very tired, as if she had not slept much, but she greeted him cheerfully.

"Hallo. I was going to bring you up some tea as soon as I'd got rid of this clutter, but I'll make it for you here in a moment if you'd like to wait."

It would have embarrassed Andrew to tell her that he had come prowling into the kitchen, looking for cheese, so he resigned himself to doing without it. It embarrassed him too that he had omitted to put on his slippers, particularly as he now saw that there was a small hole in the toe of one of his socks.

"So there's still no Laycock," he said.

"I'm afraid not," she answered. "It rather looks as if we've seen the last of him." She closed the dishwasher on all the things she had stacked inside it and set it going. Then she filled a kettle, plugged it in and started putting out cups and saucers on the table. "I hope you slept well."

"Like a log," he said. "And you?"

"No, I can't say I did, although I'd taken one of my sleeping pills. I don't often take them, but I've always had some by me since Eustace died, because for weeks after that happened I hardly slept at all, but now I only take them when something's upset me badly. And yesterday really wasn't a nice day, was it? But the pill didn't work. That's to say, when I did get off to sleep at last I had most horrible dreams. I can't remember now what they were about, I only know they were horrible."

She took a tray from a shelf, put an embroidered tray cloth on it, then a teacup, milk jug and a small silver teapot, and when the kettle boiled made tea in the little pot. She also made tea in a larger pot on the table.

"Help yourself," she said. "I'll just take this up to Felicity, then come down and join you."

She carried the tray out of the kitchen.

As she went Andrew darted a look at the refrigerator, wondering if there was a chance, if he made a rapid search, that he might find some cheese in it and be able to satisfy his craving before Agnes returned. Why not, after all? Even if she returned before he had finished searching and caught him at it, he had only to admit to a very harmless foible. He might even attempt to convince her that she herself might benefit by starting her busy day with a little piece of Stilton.

He stood up, took a step towards the refrigerator, then stood still.

From upstairs there had come a fearful crash. He recognized the sound of breaking china and heard one sharp, shrill cry.

He ran to the stairs and from the bottom of them saw that Felicity's bedroom door was open.

Then he heard Agnes calling. "Professor! Professor!"

He leapt up the stairs as fast as he could and reached the open door. Agnes was standing just inside it. She had let the tray fall to the floor. The cup and the milk jug were broken and tea was spilled over the cream-coloured carpet.

Beyond the stain of the tea Felicity lay sprawled, her eyes staring, her face a yellowish grey, her limbs rigid. She had been dead, Andrew realized almost at once, for several hours.

CHAPTER FIVE

The police arrived fifteen minutes after Andrew's call to them. He had hurried into some clothes by then, but had not shaved. The first to come were two uniformed men in a car. After them a number of others arrived, of whom the most senior was Chief Superintendent Theobald, whom Andrew had heard Felicity mention as having been in charge when she and Derek had gone to identify the body of Margot Weldon.

Felicity had not been impressed by him. He was a smaller man than most of the others who crowded into the house, a quiet, retiring-looking man with a pale, sharp-featured face, straight, light brown hair and grey eyes that never seemed to dwell on anything for more than a moment. Yet in that moment they gave the impression of taking in more than most people would be able to observe in even the longest, most thoughtful gaze. Andrew thought that Felicity had been mistaken about him when she said that he had no presence.

As soon as Andrew had made the telephone call that had brought the police Agnes had insisted on calling Felicity's doctor. Andrew had told her that this would be pointless, since nothing could be done for her and they might just as well wait until the police surgeon arrived, but she had taken the telephone over from him and called Dr. Jay. He had replied to her that he would come to the house immediately and in fact had reached it only a few minutes before the two constables in the car.

After one look at Felicity he had come out of her room and said to Agnes that it was obvious that he must not touch anything, but that he would wait until the man in charge arrived. When Superintendent Theobald appeared, his voice soft, his hands in his pockets, his stride slow and lounging, he spoke briefly to Agnes and Andrew, then asked the doctor to accompany him up to Felicity's room.

It was only then that Andrew telephoned Derek Silvester. It had been at the back of his mind that he would have to do this ever since he had looked past Agnes and the tea stain on the floor at Felicity lying stiffening there. But he had had a hope that Agnes might undertake making the call and had put off doing it himself until she actually said to him, as if of course it was for him to do it, "Aren't you going to tell Derek what's happened?"

He nodded reluctantly, asked her what Derek's number was and dialled.

A woman's voice answered.

"Mrs. Silvester?" he asked.

"No, it's Georgina," the voice answered. "Do you want my mother?"

"It's actually Dr. Silvester I'd like to speak to," Andrew said.

"I'll get him. Who is it speaking?"

"Andrew Basnett."

"Oh, that's Professor Basnett whom we met at Felicity's yesterday, isn't it?" the girl said. "Wasn't it awful—what I did, I mean? And it was only a joke, but the family will hardly speak to me now. Is Felicity ill or something, wanting my father at this hour? She isn't actually a patient of his, you know. She usually has Dr. Jay."

"Yes, I know," Andrew said, "but it isn't a case of illness."

You could hardly call death an illness. Hadn't it been described as the cure for all ills? As he spoke he glanced at his watch and saw with surprise that it was only twenty minutes past eight. He remembered that it had been seven o'clock when he had got up to look for a piece of cheese, but it felt as if several hours had passed since then.

"All right, hold on a moment," Georgina said and he heard the sound of the telephone being put down.

A moment later it was picked up again and Derek said, "Dr. Silvester speaking."

"This is Basnett," Andrew said. "I'm afraid I've some very shocking news for you. I wasn't sure whether to telephone or to come and see you—"

"It's my mother," Derek interrupted. "What's happened to her?"

An impulse with more than a little cruelty in it came suddenly to Andrew to tell her son exactly what had happened to her. But for decency's sake he restrained it. Reminding himself, however, that he was talking to a doctor to whom death would not be startling news, he said, "She's dead. She died in the night, or perhaps yesterday evening. Mrs. Cavell and I didn't find her till this morning."

"Died?" Derek said. There was a pause, then he added, "Is that all you can tell me? Nothing about how it happened? I'll come over at once, of course, but Henry Jay's her doctor. Have you got in touch with him?"

"He's here," Andrew said. "And I ought to tell you, so are the police. The fact is, Dr. Silvester, Mrs. Cavell and I didn't like the look of things and we called them immediately. I've hardly spoken to them yet, so I can't tell you much about what happened, but I gather it wasn't a mistake to call them."

There was another pause, a longer one this time. Then in a voice that had suddenly started to shake, Derek said, "Murder . . . ? There's no doubt about it?"

"I don't think so," Andrew said.

"I see. Well—well, thank you for calling. Never a nice job, breaking bad news. I'll be over at once."

The telephone was put down.

Agnes was standing at Andrew's elbow. "He's coming, is he?"

"Yes," Andrew said.

"How did he take it?"

"I suppose much as you'd expect. A bit incredulous, a bit shaken, but very restrained. Not giving anything away at the moment."

"Not giving anything away? What should he have to give away?" There was an undertone of excitement in her voice.

"About his feelings, I meant."

"Oh, I see. For a moment I thought you meant . . ." She turned away. Going to the fireplace where yesterday's ashes still lay in the grate, she took hold of the mantelshelf with both hands and leant her head on them. "What d'you think happened, Professor Basnett?"

"I've no idea," he answered, "except that it must have happened between the time you saw her last and the time you found the kitchen door open. I spent most of that time comfortably asleep in here for I'm not sure how long. I didn't notice what the time was when you woke me."

"It was about half past eleven, I think," she said. "I'd been up to my room after my talk with Felicity and watched the late news as I'd missed the one I usually watch. Then I suddenly remembered that I hadn't locked the back door, so I came downstairs again to do that and found it wide open. And really that scared me and that's why I woke you up and you remember what we did then. And d'you remember we were very quiet so that we shouldn't disturb Felicity? But it had happened by then, hadn't it?—the murder? She was dead already. And if only I'd had the sense to lock up when I usually do, it probably wouldn't have happened at all. But as I told you, I was upset by that talk I had with her and wanted to sit down and think about it, and I simply forgot about the door."

"We'll have to tell all this to the police, I expect," Andrew said. "We've neither of us got alibis. And I've a motive of sorts. She told me she was leaving me twenty thousand pounds and perhaps that would have got left out of the will she was going to make today. Whether or not Superintendent Theobald will feel inclined to believe that I can manage without that twenty thousand will depend on the kind of man he is. Your case is rather different. It looks as if you may be going to lose—" He stopped abruptly.

She raised her head and looked at him. "What is it?"

"I've just realized I haven't put on my shoes," he said. "I think I'll go and do that." He was looking down at his feet and at the small hole in the toe of one of his socks. "I'd feel rather at a disadvantage when Mr. Theobald gets around to questioning me if I didn't. I shan't be a minute."

He went out quickly, managed to persuade the constable at the foot of the stairs to allow him to go up to his room, put on his shoes and with that, found that he felt more in command of himself.

But he had not shaved yet and when he passed a hand along his jaw it felt distinctly bristly. And as the day went on it would get worse and he might not have another opportunity as good as the one he had at the moment. Going to his bathroom, he shaved, combed his hair which he had also forgotten to do when he hurriedly got dressed, put on a tie—another of the things that he had forgotten—and feeling that he would be better able to cope with questioning by that quiet policeman, if that was what he would shortly have to endure, he went downstairs again.

Agnes had left the drawing room and he deduced that she was probably in the dining room, or one of the other rooms, talking to the superintendent. But there was another woman there, kneeling by the hearth, holding a match to the fire that she had just laid. She was a small, neat, energetic-looking woman with black hair, dressed in brown trousers and a canary-coloured jersey. She heard him come in and as flames from the paper in the fireplace went leaping up the chimney she looked round and said, "You'll be Professor Basnett."

Andrew admitted that he was.

"Poor Mrs. Silvester told me you were coming," she said. "I'm Mrs. Godfrey. I come in to help every morning, only not yesterday, because it was Good Friday. And now I come today and there's police and murder. I said to myself, 'Shall I go straight home and not get mixed up in what's not my business?' But then I said to myself, 'You never know, perhaps I can help and I wouldn't want not to help if I could.' So I come in and saw this fire wanted lighting." She stood up, brushing a smudge of ashes from her knees. "And it's not only poor Mrs. Silvester but Miss Weldon too, so the fellow at the bottom of the stairs was telling me. He's Jack Prestbury. He's a friend of my husband's. My husband works in a garage in Braden and he and Jack play darts most Saturday evenings, if Jack's free, in the Ring of Bells."

"Did you know Miss Weldon then?" Andrew asked.

"Yes, I've worked for Mrs. Silvester for a long time. Ten years, it must be. There was a couple working for her when I first come, but they retired and then Miss Weldon come. I remember the commotion there was when they found she'd been signing cheques in Mrs. Silvester's name and taking the money, though I must say, it didn't surprise me. I never trusted her. Though to tell you the absolute truth, I was kind of surprised when I heard she'd been forging anything, because you've got to be clever to be able to do that, so I'd have thought, and she wasn't clever at all. In fact, she was downright stupid. She couldn't add up a column of figures and get it right. I was always having to help sort out her accounts for her. But her just being dishonest, well, I could have guessed that. But now she's dead, poor soul, so perhaps it's not right to say such things of her."

"What do you make of Laycock?" Andrew asked, thinking

that he might gather some interesting information from this woman which would not be available from Agnes Cavell.

"Oh, him!" she said contemptuously. "Now that's something I'll never understand, why Mrs. Silvester and Mrs. Cavell took to him so. It's not even as if he's specially good-looking. Just a plain round face, like a silly sort of boy."

"Wasn't it Mrs. Silvester who took him on?" Andrew said. "Mrs. Cavell came home from her holiday and found him installed. I believe she didn't take to him at first."

"Well, yes and no," Mrs. Godfrey said.

"You mean she did like him?"

"No, what I mean is, it was really her idea, getting him. It was her put the idea into Mrs. Silvester's head of having a man in the house. She kept telling her there were so many jobs a man could do that are pretty hard for a woman, and that's quite true, but Mrs. Silvester took some persuading. And then Mrs. Cavell found some advertisements for Mrs. Silvester of men wanting this kind of work and did some telephoning for her, but they were all fixed up, or didn't suit, or something. So Mrs. Cavell went away on her holiday and while she was gone Mrs. Silvester did some telephoning herself and got this chap right away. And now he's murdered her and stolen God knows what and gone off. And I can't say I'm surprised. You could tell he wasn't straight."

"Is that what your friend Jack Prestbury told you has happened?" Andrew asked.

"No, he's said nothing about it, but it stands to reason, doesn't it?"

She picked up the pan full of ashes that she had cleared out of the grate and turned to the door.

As she did so Jack Prestbury appeared there and asked Andrew if he would come to the dining room where Chief Superintendent Theobald would like a few words with him. Andrew went to the dining room where he found the superintendent standing at the window, with his back to the room. At the sound of the door opening and closing he turned, but with an air of reluctance, as if the talk that he had had with Agnes Cavell had given him enough to be going on with and he would sooner have had some time to himself in which to think it over. But he gave Andrew a little nod of greeting, one of his swift glances, gestured to him to take a chair, then began to wander aimlessly about the room, his hands in his pockets and his manner abstracted. Andrew waited patiently, seeing no reason why it should be he who had to commence their talk.

After a little while, in his low, quiet voice, Theobald said, "I expect you want to know how Mrs. Silvester was killed. She was strangled."

"What with?" Andrew asked.

"A strong pair of hands."

"Like Margot Weldon?"

"More or less."

"A man's crime then."

"Probably, though with someone as old and frail as Mrs. Silvester it might have been done by a woman."

"Do you know when it happened?"

"Only roughly, naturally. She was seen alive by Mrs. Cavell about eleven o'clock, and she'd probably been dead for seven or eight hours when she was found."

"So she was dead by midnight?"

"At the latest. Now about that will that she was talking of changing . . ."

"Yes?" Andrew said.

"Mrs. Cavell's told me something about it. Can you tell me anything?"

"Only that Mrs. Silvester said yesterday that she intended to make a new one," Andrew answered. "I believe her solicitor will be calling here later this morning to see what her wishes were."

"And can you tell me what she intended?"

"She said she was going to leave everything she had to Mrs. Cavell."

"You yourself heard her say that?"

"Yes."

"Who else heard her?"

"Several people. Her son, Dr. Silvester. His wife. Their son. His fiancée. Their daughter."

"What about the manservant, Laycock?"

With a feeling of surprise, Andrew realized that he had forgotten Laycock, though now he remembered that the young man had emerged from the kitchen at the time when Georgina, decked out in Felicity's diamonds, had been in the doorway of Felicity's bedroom and Felicity had been making her furious denunciation of her family from the top of the staircase.

"Yes, he heard it," he said. "But I'd be very surprised if a change in her will would be of any interest to him. He's only worked for her for a few months. It's hardly likely that he'd have got anything under the old will."

"But he was there, was he? When Miss Silvester appeared, wearing her grandmother's diamonds, which I understand very much upset the old lady and apparently triggered off what happened?"

Andrew realized that Theobald had been told all this by Agnes.

"Yes," he said. "But as I was saying—"

"Yes, yes," Theobald interrupted abruptly, "I'm sure Laycock had no interest in Mrs. Silvester's will. But it may have been the first time that he saw the diamonds. And you see, they happen to be missing."

"So that's why he's disappeared!" Andrew exclaimed.

"Not necessarily." Theobald gave him one of his swift glances, then wandered off to the window again. "He's disappeared and the diamonds have disappeared, but it would be unwise at this stage to assume they disappeared together."

"But doesn't that seem probable? It explains this disappearance of his that puzzled Mrs. Silvester and Mrs. Cavell so much."

"Except that if he's a professional thief, you can be sure he's known about the existence of the diamonds since almost the first day he got here. He'd have done a quick search through the house very soon after arriving, would have found them at once, and wouldn't have stayed on then for three or four months, doing a dull job, when he could easily have made off with them quietly at a convenient moment which didn't make a murder necessary. On the other hand, if he isn't a professional, but on seeing the diamonds for the first time found he couldn't resist the temptation of taking them, you'd have to assume that something made him leave the house in the middle of the afternoon, then come back in the evening to get them, and found that meant he'd got to murder Mrs. Silvester because she caught him at it. Doesn't that sound unlikely?"

"Yet you're interested in him," Andrew said, "or you wouldn't have asked me if he was there when Mrs. Silvester made her announcement about her will."

"I'm interested in everyone who knew she was going to change it," Theobald said. "In spite of what I've just been saying, it's possible to make out a case against Laycock, but it means assuming the theft of the diamonds was only a blind." He paused, coughed, turned and came to the table and sat down facing Andrew. "I believe you gain something under Mrs. Silvester's existing will, Professor."

"So she told me," Andrew said. "Of course, I never saw the document."

"Do you know how much she intended to leave you?"

"Twenty thousand pounds, she said."

"And would she have left you that in her new will?"

"I don't know."

"Twenty thousand pounds isn't a very great sum, as things go nowadays."

"No. About the diamonds being taken only as a blind—"

"Please." Theobald raised a hand. "Sometimes my mind wanders. I speculate when I ought to be going after facts. To go back to the will—"

Andrew raised a hand in imitation of Theobald's gesture and echoed his, "Please. When you said the diamonds might have been taken as a blind, it's because you think it's possible Laycock heard Mrs. Silvester say she was going to change her will, realized that every one of the people who heard her, with the exception of Mrs. Cavell, stood to lose by it, disappeared in the afternoon to make contact with one of those people whose character he must have assessed pretty accurately by then to dare to do it, arranged with that person that he'd murder Mrs. Silvester before she could make the new will, came back in the evening, killed her and took the diamonds to make it look as if the theft had been the motive for her murder. Wasn't that what you were going to say?"

A smile briefly lit up the detective's pale, reserved face. "It's a pleasure to talk to you, Professor. And I think I know what's coming next. You're going to point out that it lets you off the hook."

"Well, it does, doesn't it?"

"Because your twenty thousand wouldn't last long, paying Laycock the blackmail he'd be able to get out of you? No doubt you're right. If there's anything in this theory I've been exploring in my own mind, we've got to look for someone who'll gain rather more than you by Mrs. Silvester's death. But talking of blackmail, you haven't forgotten, have you, that we've two murders on our hands, Mrs. Silvester's last night, and Margot Weldon's on Thursday evening?"

"And you think they're connected?"

"Possibly, possibly not. It would be rash to make up our minds about it yet. But what I was going to tell you was that that letter we found in Margot Weldon's handbag, which confessed to the murder of Mrs. Silvester, which hadn't happened yet, is a forgery. She never wrote it."

Andrew sat up a little straighter in his chair. "You're certain of that?"

Theobald nodded. "We found a shopping list in the handbag and one or two odd notes which she'd certainly written herself, and our experts say there's no question about it, the letter's a forgery."

"You know she was sacked by Mrs. Silvester for forging her signature on her cheques, don't you?" Andrew said.

Theobald nodded again. "And so you're going to say that perhaps it wasn't Margot Weldon who did those forgeries, but this other character who put the letter in her handbag. That she handed in the cheques to the bank, but that was all."

Andrew gave a wry smile. "It's a pleasure to talk to you, Superintendent. Do we both go in for mind reading?"

"There's just one thing I'd like to add to that," Theobald said, "and that's the fact that whoever really forged the cheques was in Margot Weldon's power, and it was because of that that I mentioned blackmail a moment ago. She may have been bleeding him white ever since, which would supply a motive for her murder."

To his surprise, as he left the dining room, Andrew found that he had enjoyed his talk with the chief superintendent. Possibly that indicated callousness. This was not a time to enjoy anything at all. But he could not help experiencing some degree of pleasure at conversing with a man whose mind seemed to be so singularly in tune with his own. He had been susceptible to that kind of pleasure for most of his life, whether it came when he was in contact with a first-year student or a long retired, white-haired emeritus professor, more aged, more withdrawn from the active world than he was himself. However, before he left the room he was questioned carefully as to his whereabouts at the time of both murders and he could not produce a satisfactory alibi for either. Felicity, who might have been able to say that he had been with her at the time when the police believed Margot Weldon had been murdered, was unable to speak up for him, and all that he could say about what he had been doing when she herself had probably been killed was that he had nodded off to sleep in a chair by the fire.

He told Theobald of having seen Margot Weldon at Paddington, then in the train to Braden and then again at Felicity's gate on Thursday afternoon, and notes were taken of what he said and he was thanked for being so helpful, then he was allowed to leave. As he went to the drawing room he paused and briefly greeted Derek Silvester, who was being ushered into the dining room by Jack Prestbury, then the door closed on Derek and Andrew went on to the other room.

He found that besides Derek, Frances, Quentin, Georgina and Patricia had arrived. He sensed that they had been engaged in a fierce discussion before he appeared, which was broken off abruptly as he came into the room, leaving them all sitting awkwardly silent. They all looked at him questioningly, as if they expected him to have something to tell them, but all he could think of saying was "Good morning."

It took Frances a moment to have the presence of mind to say, "It's terrible, just terrible, isn't it? I still can't really believe it."

"Professor Basnett, is it true about the diamonds?" Georgina demanded.

"That they've been stolen?" he said. "Apparently."

"You see!" she cried, looking round on the others as if she had scored a point. "Didn't I always say she ought to keep them in the bank? Didn't I always say it was crazy to keep them here?"

"We all said that," Quentin said. "You weren't the only genius among us."

"But she hadn't left them to you," Georgina said. "You didn't really care what happened to them."

"And now they're all you care about," he said. "You don't really care that she's been murdered."

"Do you?" she said. "Haven't you been saying for the last year or two that she couldn't live much longer and how useful it would be if she didn't?"

"I never said anything of the kind," he said. "Anyway, not seriously. We all said that kind of thing. And none of us dreamt that the poor old thing would be murdered."

"Children, children!" Frances cried. "Don't talk like that! Don't quarrel now of all times."

"Do they quarrel much?" Patricia asked in a tone of calm interest. "I've never thought of Quentin as quarrelsome."

"They've quarrelled all their lives," Frances said. "I'm sure I don't know why. Isn't there some phrase for it psychologists use—sibling something or other? I know it somehow makes one feel it's all the parents' fault. Psychologists always do that. They blame everything on the parents instead of ever saying the children were just born like that. I can't think of anything Derek or I ever did to make the two of them so quarrelsome. I mean, we always treated the two of them just the same, we never favoured one more than the other."

"Darling Ma, don't you understand Georgina and I are devoted to one another?" Quentin said. "Our quarrelling is just the way we show it."

"You've never quarelled with me," Patricia said, "so perhaps you aren't as devoted to me as you say." It was said lightly, but her eyes were serious.

"Balls!" Georgina said. "He's so devoted to me that if I'm murdered tonight he'll only think that that will double his legacy, as I suppose it would. I don't understand the legal side of those things. Professor Basnett, do you think the diamonds were insured, and if they were, will I get the insurance money or will that go into the estate as a whole?"

"I'm afraid I don't know anything about it," Andrew answered. "I imagine they were insured, but whether for what they're worth now or only years ago, when I suppose Felicity took out the policy, I couldn't say. Their value, of course, will have increased immensely in recent years." He was wondering where Agnes was and what she was doing.

"Oh dear, isn't that awful?" Georgina said. "I mean, not to know. It isn't that I care—I mean, just about the money—I do care about Felicity. I did love her, though she never believed I did. But not knowing where one is, that's awful."

"The money's all you care about, that's obvious," Quentin said. "And you can be glad Felicity died last night, because if she'd lived till today, she'd have changed her will, leaving everything to Agnes, and you might not have got your beloved diamonds."

"Children, children!" Frances said hopelessly.

"In the circumstances, isn't it lucky you all have alibis for yesterday evening?" Patricia said. For some reason at that moment, hearing her quiet voice, Andrew became convinced that she would never marry Quentin. She had withdrawn herself from the family group, as if she had just discovered that she wanted to be no part of it. "We were all together through the evening and the police won't be able to argue with that."

"And what about the evening before when Margot was killed?" Georgina asked. "You and Quentin went out for a walk, didn't you? Are you going to be able to prove where you were?"

"As a matter of fact, we didn't go out," Quentin said. "We started out, but the gale was so fierce, we turned back. Tricia went to her room to lie down—she had a headache—and I did some work I'd brought down with me and stayed in my room till Felicity rang up about Margot and her peculiar letter. So neither of us has an alibi for Thursday evening and I'm curious if you have, Georgina. Just what were you doing? Mother and father were out playing bridge—if they really were. Darling Ma, what were you doing on Thursday evening? Were you really playing bridge with the Blakes?"

"I don't know how you can talk of that, making a joke of everything," Frances said. "Of course we were."

"Even if you weren't, you know, you won't have to give evidence against one another," Quentin said. "Husbands and wives don't have to. But what were you doing, Georgina?"

"As a matter of fact, I spent a good deal of the evening having a nice long telephone call to Marcus," she said. "I had the sitting room to myself, so I thought I could do it comfortably without being interrupted. And you can check with him that I did it."

"You mean you rang up that awful young man you've got tangled up with," Frances said, "and talked to him on *our* telephone, putting it on *our* bill, for half the evening? Oh, you children, when are you going to become a little responsible?"

"Well, it wasn't for quite as long as that," Georgina said, "but for quite a time. I should think it would give me a perfect alibi."

"Except that who's going to believe a word he says?" Quentin asked. "A little perjury wouldn't worry someone like him."

"Anyway, I don't see that it matters," Georgina said. "We've all got alibis for yesterday evening, when Felicity, whom we've all got motives for wanting dead, was killed. And though we've none of us got much in the way of alibis for Thursday evening, when Margot was killed, none of us has a motive for murdering her. So that's all right."

The door opened and Agnes came in. She was carrying a tray with cups and a pot of coffee on it. Derek Silvester followed her into the room and behind him came Jack Prestbury, who requested Mrs. Silvester to come to the dining room for a few words with Chief Superintendent Theobald. As she went she looked flustered and scared, but that, Andrew thought, was how she would look if a custard that she was making had curdled or a towel had not been returned by the laundry.

Agnes put the tray down and said, "I thought we'd all like coffee."

"Excellent," Derek said. "Just what I was wanting."

"They're making a terrible mess in the kitchen," she said. "Spreading that powder they use everywhere, looking for fingerprints. And of course they're doing it in Felicity's room and up in Laycock's room too. I suppose it's inevitable that they should suspect him."

She started pouring out the coffee.

"Why, don't you believe they should?" Quentin asked.

"Oh, I don't know," she answered. "Just a feeling I've got about him. I realize, of course, he must have been hiding something, but I liked him, you see. He helped me a great deal." She began handing the cups round. "He was always courteous and good-tempered."

"Crooks often are, I imagine," Quentin said. "I should say good manners are a con man's stock-in-trade."

"But he wasn't just a con man," Georgina said. "He was a thief and a murderer."

"You've no evidence he was either," Derek said. "All you really know against him is that he took it into his head to disappear at a very unfortunate time. You shouldn't throw accusations like that around when you don't actually know anything about the matter."

Agnes gave him a grateful smile. "I'm glad you feel like that, Derek. Things do look so black against him, it makes me want to take his side. I think he may have done something silly and irresponsible, but I can't believe it's anything really bad."

"I wish we knew a little more about him," Georgina said. "Since Felicity engaged him all by herself, he's just a blank to us."

"He's at least got an alibi for the time of Margot Weldon's murder," Andrew said. "He was with his girl friend, a Miss Bartlemy."

"Do the police believe that?" she asked.

"You can't expect me to read their minds," he answered.

Yet as he said it he thought how near he and Theobald

seemed to have come to being able to do just that. It would be
interesting to see if it continued. Probably it would not, he
thought with some regret, for there would be a good deal of
fascination in establishing a telepathic relationship with a senior detective engaged in a murder inquiry.

After Frances, Quentin was called into the dining room to
be questioned, and after him Georgina. It seemed to be felt
that there was no need to question Patricia by herself, for after
Georgina returned to the drawing room, Theobald followed
her in.

A few minutes before that, Arthur Little, Felicity's solicitor,
had arrived. He was a small man of about fifty with a smooth,
oval face, neat features and a high-domed, smoothly bald
head. His voice was low but very distinct. He appeared to have
had no knowledge of the murder until he arrived at the house
and found the entrance blocked by police cars. He stated in the
drawing room that he was appalled, astonished, grieved and
eager to give any assistance that was in his power. Then he
accepted one of the drinks which by then had replaced the
coffee that Agnes had brought in earlier and fastened a bright,
steady stare on Andrew, as if he found him the person there
whose presence most needed explaining.

When Theobald and Andrew had been introduced to him
the solicitor said, "Mrs. Silvester asked me yesterday to come
here this morning. She told me she intended to change her
will, but she didn't tell me what she wanted to do. I advised
her against it. I said that I thought her existing will was emi-
nently sensible, that it had been the result of careful thought
and that it was fair to everyone concerned. She only said, 'You
don't know what I know.' Naturally, as we talked, I never
dreamt that she would be dead by morning. I didn't even know
she was dead till I arrived here some minutes ago. A terrible
thing. I still haven't really taken it in.

"I read in *The Times* about that affair the day before, but
except for reflecting that the road across the common where

the body of that unfortunate woman was found was near to Mrs. Silvester's house, I never thought of connecting it with her. I assumed a sexual assault perhaps. But I gather you do connect the two events, so a sexual assault, I presume, does not come into the picture."

Theobald shook his head. "That's something we can leave out. But I've been trying to find out something about Margot Weldon which I believe is important, yet we seem to be up against a blank wall. Perhaps you can help us, Mr. Little. Cast your mind back several years and see if you can remember anything about how Miss Weldon got her job with Mrs. Silvester. For instance, did she ever tell you who recommended the woman to her?"

The little lawyer passed a hand over his high, smooth forehead, as if there were still hair there which he was brushing back from his brow.

"I'm sure she never mentioned it to me," he said. "She sometimes did talk over that sort of thing with me. I remember she told me that Dr. and Mrs. Silvester were anxious that she should move into a home but that she was refusing to contemplate that. Until then, she'd had a couple to look after the house for her and she was still very active herself and didn't need any personal service, but they'd decided to retire and later she told me she'd engaged a housekeeper-companion to take their place and she seemed very satisfied with the way it was working out. But then of course, there came the trouble of that woman's dishonesty—I imagine you've been told about that—how she forged some cheques of Mrs. Silvester's and was dismissed. Mrs. Silvester was very anxious that no other action should be taken and again the question came up of whether it might not be best for her to move into a home. But she was adamant against it and then she was fortunate enough to engage Mrs. Cavell, which, as we all know, has turned out admirably for several years."

"Concerning those forgeries," Theobald said, "have you ever had any doubts that they were the work of Miss Weldon?"

"Why, no, she admitted it herself, I believe," Arthur Little said. "There was no possible doubt of it."

"I asked that," Theobald said, turning so that he could take a quick look round the whole room, "because of something I told Professor Basnett, but have not yet told anyone else. The letter that was found in Miss Weldon's handbag, confessing to Mrs. Silvester's murder, is a forgery. Compared with some other specimens of her writing which were found in her hand-bag and which were certainly hers, there's no doubt of it. She didn't write that letter. So the question naturally arises, did she forge the cheques? Have we two forgers at work here? Or was there only one who forged those cheques and only got her to cash them at the bank, but then found himself in her power and that he'd got to pay blackmail to keep her silent? She'd remained in contact with someone in these parts, we can be fairly sure, or why did she come down to Braden on Thursday? And she nearly made up her mind to come to see Mrs. Silvester on Thursday afternoon. Suppose that was to tell her who the real forger had been, perhaps because he was getting behindhand with his payments. But unfortunately for her, she changed her mind and we may guess made one more attempt to come to terms with her victim, a fatal blunder which resulted in her death." He paused. "You understand, this is all fumbling in the dark. It's no more than exploring possibilities. But I thought I'd put this very hypothetical case to you in case it somehow jogs a memory in any of you. Because we want very much to find out all we can about Margot Weldon. We have her address. She lived in a bed-sitting-room in Fulham and worked as a receptionist in a small private hotel. But that's all we know about her."

There was a silence. There was no sign of response on any of the faces which his swiftly moving gaze surveyed. With a slight shrug of his shoulders, he turned to the door. At that

moment Frances exclaimed, "D'you know, it's an extraordinary thing, but it's just come back to me. I believe I was the
person who recommended Margot to Felicity."

Her husband turned on her. "That's nonsense! You never
knew anything about her."

"No, that's quite true, I didn't," Frances said. "And I quite
forgot all about it when we discussed it. But I remember a talk
I had with Felicity about that time. She was in a very bad
humour. She said you and I were trying to hustle her into a
home just to get rid of her, and she said people who went to
live in homes nearly always died a few months after they got
there. I don't know where she got that idea, but she believed it.
And so to calm her down I told her I'd heard of a woman who
might come to live with her and I'd see if I could find her
address, because I thought I'd made a note of it somewhere, in
case it should be useful, though I couldn't remember for sure if
I'd really done it or only meant to."

"That's all nonsense." Derek raised his voice as if to drown
anything more that she might have to say. "You're muddled.
You always get muddled. You're thinking of Agnes. We found
Agnes for her, but we never knew anything about how she got
hold of the Weldon woman."

"But I remember it perfectly clearly now," Frances insisted,
"though I don't suppose I've thought about it for years. I was
so worried at the way Felicity thought going into a home
would kill her and that that was what you and I were hoping
for, that I know I went searching through the drawers of my
writing table to see if I could find a bit of paper where I'd
noted down Margot's name and address in case it should come
in useful. And I suppose I found it, because of course Felicity
took Margot on, though I can't be definite about it. I've a
dreadful memory."

"The odd thing is, Dr. Silvester," Andrew said, "that your
mother herself was convinced it was you who recommended

Margot Weldon to her. She told you so yesterday. She'd an idea Miss Weldon might have been a patient of yours."

"And I told her that was nonsense." Derek's smooth, bland face reddened. "I did have a kind of feeling we'd talked about it on the telephone—whether or not my mother should go ahead and employ her or something like that. And I said Quentin or Georgina might have discovered her, but when I asked them about it, as you'll remember, they both said they hadn't, and that's good enough for me."

"But don't you understand, dear," Frances said, "it was I who told you about Margot, and you rang up Felicity and told her about her? It's quite simple."

"Except that we don't know where you got her name or if any of this is true." His tone was fierce. "For God's sake, don't try to make things more confused than they are already."

"I'm only doing my best to help clear things up," she said earnestly. "It's funny how well I remember hunting for that piece of paper in my writing table and yet can't remember who gave it to me—oh, wait a moment!" She put both hands to her head, pressing her temples as if it might help to squeeze out a thought that was not quite clear to her. "Yes, of course, it was Max Dunkerley. I said so to Felicity, didn't I? I'm almost certain it was Max."

"Was it or wasn't it?" her husband shouted at her.

"Please don't speak to me like that," she said plaintively. "How can I possibly be certain about something that happened so long ago and that didn't seem in the least important at the time? But I know Max wanted to help with the problem of finding help for Felicity. He didn't agree with us that a home would be the best thing for her. He thought she was too independent to be happy anywhere but here."

"May I ask," Theobald interrupted quietly, "who is Max Dunkerley?"

Quentin answered, "He was a very old friend of my grandmother's. He lives in Coram Court, that block of flats near the church. And it happens he's an artist of sorts, and don't artists sometimes make very competent forgers? You know, Mr. Theobald, I think my mother may have come up with something. If I were you, I'd investigate the possibility of a connection between Margot Weldon and Max Dunkerley."

CHAPTER SIX

Theobald nodded gravely. "I shall certainly do so."

He took a step towards the door, but then he paused.

"About Edward Laycock . . ." He paused again.

"I've told you, I don't think any of us know anything to speak of about him," Derek said. "My mother engaged him by herself without consulting anyone."

Andrew thought that it was time that he tried to be useful. "As a matter of fact, she told me yesterday that she had the telephone number of the woman who gave him a reference, written down in an address book. She said it was Lady Something, but she couldn't remember the name."

Theobald turned to Agnes. "Do you know anything about this address book, Mrs. Cavell?"

"Well, she had a little address book that she kept in her handbag," she answered. "That's the only one I know of."

"And do you know where the handbag is?"

"In her room, I expect." She looked round vaguely. "It isn't in here. She must have taken it upstairs with her."

Theobald went to the door and spoke to someone in the hall.

As he returned, Andrew said, "I ought to add that Mrs. Silvester told me that this woman, whatever her name is, was leaving for Canada, so you may find it difficult to make contact with her."

Theobald nodded. "That doesn't altogether surprise me."

"You don't believe in her?" Andrew asked.

"I wouldn't go so far as to say that," Theobald replied, "but we'll be wise, I think, to take everything we've learnt about Laycock with a touch of caution."

"Mrs. Silvester also told me that this woman said Laycock had worked for her for three years and given complete satisfaction," Andrew said.

"Ah well, it may be true." Theobald did not sound as if he believed for a moment that it was.

The door opened and Jack Prestbury came in. He held out a handbag to Theobald.

"Is this what you wanted, sir?" he asked. "It was on the chest of drawers in the bedroom."

Theobald spoke to Agnes again. "Would this be the handbag Mrs. Silvester was probably using yesterday?"

It was a capacious leather handbag, fairly worn, though it looked as if it might have been smart in its day.

Agnes nodded. "Probably. It's the one she used most of the time, unless she'd dressed for some special occasion and wanted one that would match her outfit. You'll find those in the chest of drawers in her room. But I'm sure this is the one she'd been using for general purposes recently."

He handed the bag to her. "Would you mind looking for the address book?"

She opened the bag which seemed to be bulging with a note-case, a change purse, a cheque book, keys and all the things that collect in a woman's handbag. She explored it with a frown deepening on her face.

After a moment she said, "I can't find it."

Theobald took the bag from her and looked through its contents himself.

"What's the book like?" he asked.

"It's just an ordinary little address book, pale blue, I think, full of all sorts of names, a good many of them people who've been dead for years. She'd just cross those out and sometimes she'd say it was time she got a new book and copied the remaining people in, but I don't think she ever got around to it."

"And she always kept it in this handbag?"

"So far as I know."

"She wouldn't have taken it out and left it, say, on her writing table, if she'd been going to write some letters?"

"I suppose that's possible."

"But you don't think it's likely."

She was looking agitated. "I simply don't know. It isn't a thing I ever thought about. I just know she had this little blue book and if Mrs. Silvester told Professor Basnett she'd written down that woman's telephone number in it, I suppose she had, but she never said anything about it to me. And I can't imagine why the book should be missing.

Theobald looked as if he thought that he could make a good guess as to why it should be, but without saying anything further he went once more to the door, went out and again spoke to someone in the hall. Then he returned.

"I think we must do our best to find this book," he said. "If she'd taken it out of her handbag, as I suggested, because she was writing letters, where would she have done that?"

Agnes nodded at a bureau in a corner of the room. Its flap was open and its pigeonholes were jammed with writing paper, envelopes and letters answered and unanswered. No small blue book was visible.

A soft cough from a corner of the room reminded the people in it of the presence of Arthur Little, the solicitor.

"If it's because of that lady's address that you're anxious about the book, Mr. Theobald," he said, "I believe I may be able to help you."

"You've got it?" Theobald asked.

"I can't answer that offhand," Arthur Little said, "but I think we may have a note of it in our office. As I told you, Mrs. Silvester sometimes did discuss her personal affairs with me, and I remember, when she was thinking of engaging Laycock, she rang me up and asked me what I thought of the idea. The idea of her taking on a manservant, I mean. I believe if

Mrs. Cavell hadn't been away, she'd simply have discussed it
with her and wouldn't have wanted to talk it over with me, but
it was as if she felt she'd like to consult someone before going
ahead with the scheme. So I told her I thought it was an
excellent idea if she checked the man's references carefully first
and she then told me the lady's name and telephone number
and I was under the impression that she wanted me to check
the reference for her, so I wrote it down. But almost immediately she said that she would do it herself, but I think I may
have kept my note of the name in her file. I can't say for sure I
have, but if I can be of no further use here, I'll go to the office
and ascertain whether I did or not. I understand it's a matter
of some urgency."

"Thank you, Mr. Little, if you'd do that it would be very
helpful," Theobald said. Then as the solicitor went out, he
added, "In the meantime, Mrs. Cavell, I think we should start
a search for this book. Have you, or you, Dr. Silvester"—he
turned to Derek—"any objection?"

"No," Derek said. "Go ahead."

"Of course," Agnes said.

"As a matter of fact," Frances said in her soft, hesitant
voice, "I've a sort of idea I've just remembered the woman's
name. It suddenly popped into my head. But I may be quite
wrong. I mean, it may be connected with something quite different, some committee I'm on or something, and not have
anything to do with Felicity at all. But I believe she did talk
about it once anyway, and now this name's come suddenly
into my mind. Lady Graveney. Of course I don't know anything about her telephone number. I don't suppose Felicity
mentioned it. But as I told you, my memory's terrible."

Andrew was beginning to feel that Frances's memory was a
good deal better than that of anyone else in the room and from
the look that Theobald gave her, he thought that the same idea
had occurred to the superintendent. But again Theobald left

the room to issue orders for a search through the house for the little address book.

Theobald raised no objection when Derek suggested that he and his family should go home, and that made Andrew wonder for a moment if there would be any objection to his returning home also. He almost suggested it. After all, Braden-on-Thames was only a short distance from London. He could be reached on the telephone and recalled in only an hour or two if it should turn out unexpectedly to be necessary.

The thought seemed almost unbearably attractive. To be in his quiet flat, to be alone, to be able to do a little work on his life of Robert Hooke, to be free of any responsibility to anybody, to be free of these busy policemen and the mood of fear and suspicion that somehow attended them, to forget, if only that were possible, that he had ever known a woman called Felicity, how splendid that would be. But he had only to take one look at Agnes Cavell to know that he was not at all serious about trying to make good his escape. He could not leave her alone here.

She was sitting in a chair by the fire while a young detective whom Theobald had brought in sat at the bureau in a corner of the room and went methodically through the drawers and pigeonholes. She looked so forlorn that Andrew longed to be able to say something to comfort her. There was colour in her face and her eyes seemed to have become enormous, with a fixed, unseeing glitter in them. But it felt impossible to talk while the young man was there. All that Andrew could think of doing was pouring out drinks for her and for himself. But although Agnes accepted the glass that he gave her, she almost immediately put it down on the table beside her and did not touch it.

Andrew, after a few sips, did the same. He had an uncomfortable feeling that if he was not careful, this was one of the rare occasions on which he might easily get drunk. He wondered what Agnes intended to do about lunch. He had had no breakfast and was beginning to feel very hungry. But it seemed to him possible that in her present mood she might simply have forgotten that food, even in a time of great strain, is on the whole a good thing. If she showed no sign of taking some action about it soon, he would go out to the kitchen and see what he could do about it himself. He could no doubt find eggs and make omelets for them both.

However, he waited until the detective had finished at the bureau and had wandered round the room, opening drawers in every piece of furniture that had them, then with a word of apology for his intrusion, went out. As soon as she had gone Agnes bent forwards, hid her face in her hands and broke into violent sobs. Her whole body shook with them. The sound of them was like a child's frantic, unrestrained crying. Andrew, moved, embarrassed, anxious to be kind but feeling hopelessly inadequate, went rigid in his chair, not knowing what to do. Then absentmindedly he swallowed a good deal of his whisky.

It at least gave him back the power of speech. "You were very fond of Felicity then," he said.

It did not sound to him a very helpful thing to say, but it seemed to remind her that he was there. She gulped a few times, groped for a handkerchief in a pocket and mopped her eyes.

After a little while, in a shaky voice, she asked, "What do you think?"

"You must have been," he said.

"What makes you think that?"

It was not what he had expected. He thought that her explosion of tears told all that it was necessary to know about that.

"I don't think you're a person who cries easily," he said. "It's taken a good deal of grief to make you break down like that."

"Grief isn't the only thing that makes one cry," she said.

"What else is there?"

"Oh, anger, disappointment, fear—all kinds of things."

She sat back in her chair, gazing vacantly up at the ceiling, her handkerchief clasped in her fist.

"And are you angry, disappointed or afraid?" he asked.

"All three of them," she said. "Don't you understand that?"

"I'm afraid not," he answered. "Who are you angry with, apart from the brute who murdered Felicity, and I'd say that that really comes under the heading of grief."

"Oh, all the Silvesters, and you too."

"I'm sorry if I've made you angry. What have I done?"

"You've done nothing, that's what you've done. You've all done nothing. You've let the police believe that poor boy Ted is responsible for everything, yet you haven't come up with the slightest suggestion of a motive. Yet here they are, turning the house upside down, looking for that wretched address book. But why should Ted have killed Felicity? For her diamonds? He could have taken them any time without killing her. And don't you believe her murderer came to the house on Thursday evening after dumping Margot Weldon's body in the road across the common, and opened the back door and let in that draught you and Felicity talked about, then went away because he realized she wasn't alone? That was your own idea, wasn't it? Yet we know Ted couldn't have done that. He was with his girl friend. I asked that man Theobald about that today and he said the girl confirms what Ted said. So someone is lying, isn't that obvious? And I'm very angry with that person, even if he isn't the murderer."

Andrew wondered for a moment if he should tell her of Theobald's theory that Laycock might have murdered Felicity to oblige some member of the Silvester family who was scared by her threat that she would change her will, but he decided to keep it to himself.

"I haven't told any lies so far," he said, "but of course there's no reason why you should believe me."

"Oh, I believe you," she said indifferently. "The truth is,

I'm angry with everybody and everything, including myself. I ought to have seen all this coming."

"How could you have done that?"

"I don't know. I don't know anything. It's just a feeling I have. Life has been so smooth and comfortable recently and that's always dangerous. One should never forget how easily it can all be ruined."

"You only think that because today's been so terrible," Andrew said. "Grief hits us in all kinds of ways. You must have cared for Felicity very much."

"Grief, grief!" Springing to her feet, she suddenly shouted the word at him. "I'm not grieving for Felicity! I never cared for her. She was a vain, selfish old woman who used her money to dominate people in the way she'd used her beauty when she was younger. She never loved anyone herself or gave any part of herself to anyone. I haven't been crying for her. I've been crying for myself. I've been crying out of disappointment, bitter, bitter disappointment. You didn't really believe I don't care about that money, did you? You didn't believe I wouldn't have fought tooth and nail to keep it. I said I wouldn't because it was the nice thing to say, the kind of thing nice, kind Agnes Cavell might be expected to say. But it wasn't true. How could it be true? Of course I wanted the money, all of it, and I so nearly got it. That's what's so unbearable. I so nearly got it. So now you know what I'm really like and you can make what you want out of it."

She darted to the door and out of the room. Andrew heard her footsteps running up the stairs.

The police did not leave the house until about three o'clock in the afternoon. Andrew, growing hungrier and hungrier, had made one or two sorties into the kitchen to see if he could find something to stave off the pangs, but there had always been one or two men there, doing he was not sure what, except that once, he thought, he had almost caught one of them helping himself surreptitiously to something out of the refrigerator. When at last they all left some time after Felicity's body had been removed in an ambulance, he went out to the kitchen again and finding some cold beef in the refrigerator, made a thick sandwich for himself, returned to the drawing room, made up the fire and settled down beside it to enjoy food and drink and the mere silence in the house.

He had thought of calling up to Agnes that he would make her a sandwich if she would like one, but something about the untouched glass of whisky on the table beside the chair where she had sat made him feel that the best thing that he could do for her was to leave her alone. If she wanted food, she could come and get it.

Eating his own sandwich with satisfaction, he thought about how incompetent he was at understanding other people. When he had heard Agnes declare that she truly did not want Felicity to leave her money to her, that if the other Silvesters brought an action against her she would not dream of fighting it, he had believed without question that she was sincere and had admired her for it. Yet now she had asserted that that had been hypocrisy, that she had merely been saying the kind of thing that everyone expected her to say and that in reality she would have fought for the money tooth and nail. But had that necessarily been true? Had it been anything but a hysterical reaction to the shock and pain of the day? Had she perhaps said it out of a kind of defiance because it was what she thought he must really believe about her? He wavered between the two possibilities and ended up by recognizing that as he hardly knew the woman at all, it was unlikely that he would be able to find the correct answer to such a complex problem.

Finishing his sandwich and his whisky, he decided to go for a walk. He had no clear idea when he set out of where he intended to go and took the road into the town without thinking about it. With the capriciousness of April weather, the afternoon had turned cloudy and colder than it had been for some days, though the strong wind had not returned. Remembering as he walked along how fiercely it had blown on Thursday evening, a fact struck him which was so obvious that he wondered why he had not considered it before. It was simply that at the time when he and Felicity had both shivered and had later more than half believed that at that moment someone with murder in mind had opened the back door, Felicity had not yet said anything about changing her will and her diamonds had not disappeared.

So if the truth was that at the time of the sudden draught through the house someone who had already planted the confession to Felicity's murder in Margot Weldon's handbag and had come to follow that up by murdering Felicity, it could not have had anything to do with her will. The theft of the diamonds might have been the motive for murdering Felicity and the failure to get them that evening might have been what had brought the murderer back next day. But the will could not have had anything to do with either murder, unless the fact was that the two occurrences had nothing to do with one another.

Brooding on the possibility of this, Andrew looked around him, noticed that he was near the church and admitted to himself that this was where he had intended to come from the first. For Coram Court, where Max Dunkerley lived, he had heard was close to the church.

Andrew had not been told what street it was in, but among the old houses at the centre of the town it was easy enough to find it, a moderate-sized block of flats, four storeys high, probably built in the nineteen-thirties and now with a shabby air, not exactly dilapidated but certainly in need of a little freshening up. A coat of paint would not have come amiss. Going up to the entrance, he saw Max Dunkerley's name on a card beside one of a row of bells, rang it, heard a moment later the sound of clicking at the door, pushed it open and saw a lift facing him.

Max's flat was on the second floor. Entering the lift, Andrew pressed the second floor button and was taken shakily upwards. Max had opened the door of his flat and was waiting for him on the landing by the time that he emerged from the lift. Max was wearing an old sweater, out at elbows, and wrinkled corduroy trousers. His scanty pinkish hair curled on the roll collar of his sweater. His wide-open blue eyes contemplated Andrew with the startled look that he remembered, almost as if he were prepared to bar the way to so unexpected an intruder.

Yet he smiled, said in his high-pitched, grating voice, "Ah, it's you. A good idea to call. We can talk. Come in," and stood aside for Andrew to enter.

Andrew remembered that Felicity had called it an "unspeakable little flat." That was an exaggeration. It seemed to have only two rooms, a bedroom and a living room, besides the bathroom and the kitchen. But except that the living room, which Andrew supposed was the room that Max had called his studio, was extremely untidy, it was pleasant enough in its way. The furniture belonged to half a dozen different periods and there was rather too much of it and the walls were almost completely covered in pictures, which Andrew found oppressive and made him wonder where Felicity's pictures would be hung. But no doubt some that were here now would be sacrificed for them. There were comfortable chairs and a nice hearth rug. An easel had a half-finished seascape on it and there was a stack of canvases in a corner and several pots of green trailing plants on the windowsill. It was the room of a man who lived alone, but certainly as he chose.

Max said, "I'll make some coffee. Won't take a minute. D'you know, if you'd come an hour ago you'd have found me in tears? The police came here and told me what had happened, then asked a lot of damfool questions and I controlled myself while they were here, then cried like a child. I don't promise I shan't start again. You'll be asking the same questions, I expect, and that may set me off again. But there are one or two I'd like to ask you. Sit down. Smoke if you want to. Cigarettes on the mantelpiece."

He went out.

Andrew, who did not smoke and who was repelled by the heavy smell of stale cigarette smoke in the room and the quantity of stubs in everything that could be regarded as an ashtray, did not sit down, but roamed around the room, taking a closer look at some of the pictures on the walls. Most of them were signed with the initials "M.D.," so could be presumed to be Max Dunkerley's own work. There was nothing distinguished about them, but the sheer quantity of them showed that it must give him great pleasure to produce them.

He returned after only a few minutes with mugs and a coffeepot. Instant coffee, undoubtedly. Filling a mug for Andrew, he filled one for himself and settled down sprawling on a spindly little Victorian sofa.

"Well, go on," he said. "Ask me what you want to know."

Faced with the blunt question, Andrew found that he did not know what he wanted to say. He sat down in a worn but well-padded armchair that probably dated from the nineteen-twenties.

"I didn't come to ask anything special," he said. "I wanted to get out of the house. I wanted to get away from Mrs. Cavell who's in a very emotional state. I'm sure that sounds callous, but when you know a person's in great trouble and you realize you can't do a thing to help them, it's a natural instinct to flee. And I didn't feel any inclination to visit the Silvester family. But that reminds me . . ." He paused.

"Ah," Max said, "now you've remembered what you came to ask me. Yes?"

Andrew had almost convinced himself while he had been speaking that he had not come there to ask Max Dunkerley anything special, and it amused him, now that the other man's perception had been too quick for him, that really the question had been on the tip of his tongue.

"Mrs. Silvester—the younger one, Frances—said something this morning that interested me," he said, "and I've been wondering if there's any truth in it."

"Never believe Frances," Max said. "She's one of the most completely unreliable people I've ever come across. But perhaps you've realized that yourself."

"I've been wondering about it," Andrew said. "She seems a little muddle-minded."

"The trouble is, you know, I've never made up my mind whether that muddle-mindedness of hers, as you call it, is genuine or not," Max said. "I'm inclined to think it's an act with which she defends herself from her rather dominating family. Because Derek, as you may have noticed, likes to have his own way, and the two children, I've no hesitation in saying, are devils. Not that I'm not very fond of them both. I've known them since they were babes. But talking of Frances, I rather think the truth about her is that she's a shrewd, mildly unscrupulous woman who blames her bad memory or her state of general mental confusion if there's any risk of her being caught out, for any of the lies she may feel inclined to tell."

"So when she said she thought it was you who recommended Margot Weldon to her, after which she recommended her to Dr. Silvester and he to Felicity, you'd say it was a deliberate lie—supposing it doesn't happen to be true."

"Ah," Max said, "I see. That's what you came to ask me. Is it true?" He smiled amiably, as if there were something entertaining about being suspected.

"The question's been worrying me," Andrew confessed. "Among other things."

"I know, I know. Just how I feel myself. Everything seems a little mad." Max reached for a cigarette. "No, I didn't recommend the woman to anybody. I'd never heard of her till Felicity told me she'd employed her. And yes, if Frances says I found Margot for Felicity, I'd say that's one of her deliberate lies. But it might not be. That's one of the awful things about the woman. One can never be sure."

"Has she anything against you that explains her trying to get you mixed up in this?"

"Not that I know of. Not that it's a thing I've ever thought about. I'd have said we were quite good friends. If she's trying to involve me, I'd say it's probably because she's trying to protect someone else. One of her family, of course, who may not even need protecting. But she could have been genuinely muddled, because I did talk to her about someone, a nice elderly woman who I thought would suit Felicity, and Frances said she'd ask Derek what he thought. But then I heard that Margot had been taken on, so naturally I didn't raise the matter again."

"If it's one of her family she's protecting, which of them do you think it would be?"

"There I can't help you, I'm afraid. I'd say Quentin is her favourite. All the same, it could be any of the others. And that recommendation could have been given quite innocently and have nothing to do with the forgeries or the murders, and whoever gave it may only be keeping quiet about it now out of fear. Now I said I was going to ask you some questions. Tell me, have they found out anything about Laycock?"

Andrew drank some of his coffee. "He hasn't reappeared, if that's what you mean. But Felicity's solicitor, Arthur Little, thought he might have a note of the name and address of the woman who gave him a reference and was going to check it, but I haven't heard the result of that yet. Felicity, so she told me, talked to this woman herself and then engaged the man without any consultation with her family or Mrs. Cavell, who had gone away on holiday."

"Ah," Max said. "Yes."

"Does that mean anything special?" Andrew asked.

"I was just wondering what you make of Agnes Cavell," Max said.

There was something in his tone which made it sound as if he would be glad to be told something to her discredit.

Cautiously, Andrew replied, "She seems a very admirable woman."

"Of course, of course. Do you know, not long ago I asked her to marry me? Luckily she had the sense to refuse. It wouldn't have worked at all. But of course I haven't forgiven her. At the time I never dreamt she could possibly refuse me and I'm afraid I've never managed to trust her since. Sheer wounded vanity, of course, but there it is. I always wonder what she's thinking about when she looks at me. Such a candid, open look and I can't help thinking it hides contempt and dislike."

"I imagine it was just that she didn't want to marry anybody," Andrew said. "I believe she was very devoted to her husband."

"Yes, yes, of course, that's the obvious explanation. Sometimes I almost believe it."

"But there was something I was told this morning by Mrs. Godfrey who I understand comes in daily to help in the house, and I wonder what you think of it." Andrew finished his coffee and put his cup down.

"Something about Agnes?"

"Well, yes," Andrew said. "It was only that Mrs. Godfrey believes that it was Mrs. Cavell who put the idea of employing a manservant into Felicity's head and who then found some advertisements and tried ringing up the people who'd advertized, but had no success with them. Then she went away and soon afterwards Felicity herself tried some of this ringing up and was at once successful."

Max's hard, bright stare dwelt steadily on Andrew's face for a moment.

"I'm not sure if I understand you," he said. "What is there strange about that? Wasn't it just chance?"

"I expect so."

"But you don't think it was."

"I think it must have been."

"What's worrying you then?"

Andrew stirred uneasily. He had not really meant to talk so much.

"There's the disappearance of an address book Felicity usually kept in her handbag," he said. "She told me herself she'd a note of that woman's number in it, the one who recommended Laycock. And the police have been turning the house inside out, looking for the book, but they haven't found it. So it looks as if someone who knew there was this note in it wanted to hide the fact and removed the book, obviously to conceal something about Laycock. And the most likely explanation is that it was Laycock himself who did it, if it was he who came back to the house to do the murder. The police found the handbag in Felicity's bedroom this morning, with no book in it. But it just might have been Mrs. Cavell who took it, mightn't it? She came and went in the house. She could have got at the handbag any time. It wouldn't necessarily have had to be yesterday evening. It might have been missing for days without Felicity noticing it."

"But that argues Agnes has some connection with Laycock," Max said, "and I don't see how she could have. There's no question that she was away when Felicity took him on. She was so proud of having done it herself, you know. She wanted to display to us all that she was still perfectly independent."

"Yes, I'm only trying to think of who could have got at the handbag," Andrew said.

As he said it, he suddenly understood what had been driving him on since he had begun to talk about the address book and its mysterious disappearance. Yesterday evening, when Max Dunkerley had come to dinner, the two women had left the dining room before the men and Max and Andrew had sat on for a little while, talking of the love that Max had felt for Felicity and of the beauty that she had still had in her sixties. Then Andrew had gone to the drawing room, but Max had lingered behind, supposedly to go to the lavatory. But if he had not really done that, he would have had time to go quickly upstairs, go into Felicity's room, find her handbag and extract the address book from it.

Not that Andrew had the faintest idea why Max should have done such a thing. However, it was a possibility which perhaps should be borne in mind. It should also be borne in mind that if Max had done that, he had had an opportunity too to help himself to Felicity's diamonds. It did not occur to Andrew to speak of this, but he found himself watching Max's face with sudden alertness.

He could discern no change of expression on it.

"If Little has a note of that woman's name and address," Max said, "the theft of the book was pointless."

"Quite pointless," Andrew agreed.

"Someone must be feeling very disappointed."

"Very."

"Interesting, very interesting," Max said. "Yet it's possible, isn't it, that it wasn't that particular address this person wanted? Suppose there was something in the book that tied someone up with Margot Weldon."

Andrew had been pursuing his own line of thought so doggedly that he had not thought of this. "That's possible, of course," he said.

"Or something else, something quite innocent."

Andrew did not believe for a moment that it was innocent, but he recognized that this was not impossible and that one of the troubles about the situation in which he found himself at the moment was the temptation to assume that every little thing that had happened during the last two days was in some way connected with the two murders. The truth might be that there was an innocent explanation of nearly everything and that the main clues to the mystery, or to the two mysteries, if it turned out that they were unconnected, had yet to be revealed.

A few minutes later he left. Max accompanied him to the lift, summoned it for him and thanked him for his call and their most interesting talk. Andrew went down in the creaking lift and let himself out into the street where the streetlamps had already been lit and dusk was already deepening in the early evening. The dusk took him by surprise, yet it should not have done so, for by the time that he had left Max's flat it had been dark enough in there. But Andrew had been too engrossed in what they had been talking about to think of it.

As he walked along he found himself wondering if it was conceivable that Max had stolen the diamonds. He had had the time and the opportunity to do it. But if he had, then their theft and Felicity's death had nothing to do with one another. She had been alive and well when he had left the house. If the theft had been successfully achieved soon after dinner, what could possibly have brought him back?

It all seemed very unlikely. Yet suppose he was in urgent need of money. It was impossible to guess whether a man who lived in the kind of disorder in which Max Dunkerley chose to live was rich or poor. Hadn't someone said that he had worked for the United Nations? That meant that he must have a reasonable pension and perhaps, if he had lived most of his working life abroad, had had an untaxed income out of which he might have saved a substantial amount.

But he might be a compulsive gambler, or have relations who made sudden large demands for money on him which he felt unable to refuse, or he might even be subject to blackmail. Perhaps he needed money. Perhaps he was a thief. Perhaps he was a liar and had introduced Margot Weldon into Felicity's house. Perhaps he was a murderer . . .

"Professor Basnett! Professor Basnett!"

Andrew started. He had just passed the police station and now heard swift footsteps behind him, as if someone had just emerged from it and was running to catch up with him. Turning, he saw Patricia Neale. She had on a waterproof and had a scarf tied over her brown hair.

"I thought it was you," she said as she joined him, "and there's something I want to ask you. You're going back to Ramsden House, I suppose. Do you mind if I walk along with you?"

"It'll be a pleasure," he answered. "Have the police been questioning you?"

"I've been questioning them." She fell into step beside him as they walked on. Her hands were in her pockets and there was a worried frown on her face. "I wanted to ask them simply if I'd got to stay here or if I could go home."

"I'm sure you can go home if you want to," he said, "as long as they know how to get in touch with you."

"That's what they said. But what about you? Are you staying?"

"For the moment."

"Why?"

"Well, I thought of going home," he said, "but then I thought that leaving Mrs. Cavell to cope with everything by herself was hardly fair on her, though to tell you the truth, I'm not sure she wouldn't just as soon be left alone. You want to leave, do you?"

"Yes, but then—well, you think one ought to stay, do you?"

"Oh, I'm only speaking for myself. In your case, I suppose it depends a good deal on how Quentin feels about it."

"It doesn't really," she said, "because, you see, we aren't engaged any more. We decided to break it off this afternoon."

"I'm sorry," Andrew said.

She gave him a withering look. "Why should you be sorry? D'you know, people always say they're sorry if someone says they've broken off an engagement or decided to have a divorce? Yet it may in fact be the best thing that could have happened to them. Why can't they ever say they're delighted to hear it?"

"I'm afraid it's just automatic, to indicate one's sorry a person hasn't been as happy as one assumed. You haven't been happy?"

"We were very happy as lovers," she said. "But getting married—now that's a different thing."

"I thought it wasn't so very different nowadays," he said.

"Oh, it is. It's committing oneself, you see. Or that's how I look at it. But then if you find the person isn't quite what you thought they were, it's terribly upsetting."

He looked at her curiously. Her slightly crooked profile was set as she strode along beside him.

Mostly because he realized she needed to talk, he said, "What's wrong with Quentin?"

"His family, for one thing."

"But you don't marry a family."

"You do, in a way. You marry his relationship with his family. That's part of him. And I've never seen it before, but he seems quite a different person when he's with them. He seems to think about money almost as much as they do, and I don't really quarrel with that because of course everybody does it, but it's brought out a sort of instability in him that scares me. He's already planning what he's going to do with Felicity's legacy when he gets it. He's going to give up his job and go and live somewhere abroad and start writing again. And that isn't what I bargained for."

"You don't want to live abroad?"

"It isn't exactly that. It's just that I've realized I haven't got enough faith in him to do it. I mean, I don't think he's got the talent to justify it. He'll get through the money without achieving anything and then he'll be back where he was, needing a job but a bit older and out of touch with things . . . Oh God,

I oughtn't to be talking like this, it's horribly disloyal, because I'm really very fond of him, you know. But I did want to ask you if you thought it would look very bad if I walked out on him now. Really it would, wouldn't it? I'd better not do it."

"You think it might look as if you suspected him of being involved in these murders?" Andrew asked.

She took a moment to reply. "You understand, it's not that I *do* suspect him."

"No, of course not."

She gave him a faintly scowling look. "No, it isn't! It's just a question of how it would look. That's really why you're staying on, isn't it? It isn't really because of Agnes, it's because of how it would look if you hurried away."

"You may be right," Andrew admitted. "Incidentally, do Quentin's family know you've broken off the engagement?"

"Not yet. And that makes things a bit embarrassing. Not that it matters much, but naturally I'd like to go home. We haven't exactly quarrelled—we've been appallingly good mannered about it and ever so nice and understanding to each other—but it all feels a bit unreal. But please do tell me, do you think I ought to stay or not?"

"My dear girl, how can I possibly tell you?" Andrew began to feel impatient. Throughout his working life, when he had often been asked for advice by the young, the forlorn and the bewildered, he had never felt happy about giving it. "We hardly know each other."

"That's why I wanted to talk to you," she said. "I thought you'd be able to take an objective view of things."

"Well, I can't. And whatever I say, you know as well as I do that you'll end up working the problem out for yourself."

Instead of the scowl, he was given a sudden smile. "Of course I shall. All the same, thank you very much for letting me talk. I expect it was an awful bore for you. I'm really very grateful. Talking to the police just made me feel explosive because they gave me such suspicious looks, or that's how I felt about them anyway. But now I've really calmed down quite nicely. And this is where our roads part."

They had come to a crossroads, the road ahead being the one that would take Andrew into Old Farm Road and the turning to the right being the one, he supposed, that led towards the home of Derek Silvester's family, for it was in that direction that Patricia took a step or two. But then she paused.

"If I want to come and talk to you again, may I do it?" she asked.

"Any time, as long as you aren't hoping for words of wisdom," he said.

She gave him another smile and started off down the road.

Andrew went on to Ramsden House. He had to ring the bell to be admitted and while he waited after he had heard it peal inside, he wondered if it would be audible upstairs if Agnes happened still to be in her room, and what he should do if he could not get in. However, she opened the door almost immediately. She looked subdued but calm, quite unlike the desperate woman who had cried out at him so wildly and then gone running up to her room to hide herself. She did not speak or go into the drawing room with him, but disappeared into the kitchen from which a savoury odour of something good reached him. So she had sought stability, he thought, by returning to her normal routine of cooking. An excellent thing. He felt more than ready for a good meal.

Before it, she brought sherry into the drawing room.

In a low voice she said, "I'm very sorry about the way I behaved this afternoon. Please forget everything I said."

"Don't worry," he said. "It was natural enough."

"It won't happen again. Are you staying here, Professor Basnett, or going home?"

"Which would you prefer?" he asked.

"Whichever you prefer yourself, if the police agree to it."

"Suppose we leave it till tomorrow and see whether or not they've anything to tell us."

"Very well."

She poured out sherry for them both and sitting down, sipped hers, then closed her eyes. Nervous exhaustion had added a look of ten years to her age. Andrew did not try to talk to her and during the meal that soon followed of a very good soup, grilled chops and fruit salad and cream, they were both nearly silent.

Soon after it he went up to his room and as he had done the evening before, got into bed, switched on the table lamp beside it and resumed reading the Agatha Christie that he had started. He read for a time until he realized that he was turning the pages without having taken in a word of what was on them. To his extreme irritation, a verse began to hammer in his brain and would not be stilled.

> "When all the world is young, lad,
> And all the trees are green;
> And every goose a swan, lad,
> And every lass a queen;
> Then hey for boot and horse, lad,
> And round the world away . . ."

When he had been only eleven years old, at the time when the lines had been indelibly imprinted on his memory, he had wondered how you got round the world on a horse. Now that point seemed unimportant and it merely annoyed him that he could not stop the verse repeating itself on and on in his tired mind. The events of the day had kept him free of it, but now it was back, pounding away pointlessly in his brain.

Yet perhaps not altogether pointlessly, for once or twice during the evening he had caught himself thinking that if he was really to inherit twenty thousand pounds from Felicity, he might spend at least some of it on a second trip round the world. He had enjoyed his last trip immensely, even though he had often felt desolated by the fact that Nell was not there to enjoy it with him. He had not grown used to loneliness yet.

But the truth was that if he simply invested the money in government securities, as his habit was, it would bring in only a relatively small addition to his income, whereas spending it on something that would give him real pleasure, even if he was not young and his world not particularly green any more, would surely be of positive value.

Finding himself thinking of this, however, disgusted him. Even if he had never been fond of Felicity, he owed her more than that. So soon after her horrifying death, how could he do it? Sadly he supposed that money meant as much to him as to the people to whom he would have liked to feel superior.

Next morning he got up, as he usually did, at seven o'clock, went downstairs without concealment and helped himself to some cheese that he found in the refrigerator. Returning to his room, he had a bath, shaved and got dressed. He and Agnes breakfasted together at eight o'clock. She was still in the quiet mood of the evening before, offering him the Sunday paper and plainly hoping that he would occupy himself with it.

Because it was Sunday, Mrs. Godfrey was not to be expected, but when Andrew suggested that he should lay the fire in the drawing room, Agnes rejected the offer and proceeded to do it herself. He felt that the best thing that he could do for her was to keep out of her way as much as possible. After all, it might be best if he did not stay on, but returned to London later in the day if the police had no objection to his doing so. He could find out about that presently. The day was fine and calm and a walk down to the police station would not be disagreeable.

It turned out to be unnecessary. About ten o'clock Chief Superintendent Theobald and a young sergeant appeared. Agnes showed them into the drawing room where Andrew was sitting with the various sections of the Sunday paper scattered around him beside the fire which was now burning brightly. Theobald remarked that it was nice to see a fire nowadays, that it was a nice morning and that he hoped Mrs. Cavell and Professor Basnett had slept well. Andrew thought of certain African tribes who greet each other on meeting with fiery but actually harmless dances to show that they come in peace, and he wondered if Theobald's going through the equivalent British rituals indicated that he was not bringing trouble.

When he went on to speak Andrew was not sure at first if it meant trouble or not.

"I came to tell you that we've identified the man Laycock," Theobald said, "and I think the chances are you're lucky to be rid of him. We traced him easily by his fingerprints. He's a man who came out of prison about four months ago, after doing five years for the armed robbery of a bank in Croydon. He'd been in trouble once or twice before for relatively minor offences and done short spells in prison and he had a new name for each occasion. He's called himself Spencer and Parker and Prosser. Which of them, if any, is his real name, we don't know. But what's strange is that the one thing he's never done before is a job of work of the kind he's been doing here. It would almost look as if he'd been trying to go straight, if he and Mrs. Silvester's diamonds hadn't disappeared together."

Agnes let out a long breath. Andrew realized that she had been holding it ever since Theobald had begun to speak of Laycock.

"D'you know, I've sometimes wondered if his history mightn't be something like that," she said. "Of course I knew he wasn't what he was trying to appear. But I liked him and if he was trying to go straight, I wanted to help him. But what about his reference? How did he get it? Who was the woman Felicity talked to?"

"She's vanished into thin air, if she ever existed," Theobald said. Mr. Little says she was a Lady Graveney and we traced her address from the telephone number he'd noted down. It's a block of small furnished flats and the flat she had she took only for a month and she was joined there by a man. She's been described to us by the caretaker as a middle-aged woman with black hair and he as a round-faced and boyish-looking man a good deal younger than she was. He may or may not have been her boy friend, but it's fairly certain he was Laycock, whoever she was. We thought she just might be Margot Weldon, but when we showed the caretaker her photograph he said it was nothing like her."

"But do I understand you suspect him only of the theft of the diamonds and not of either murder?" Agnes said.

"We don't suspect him of the murder of Margot Weldon," Theobald said. "It isn't only his girl friend, Myra Bartlemy, who's a quite respectable girl who works for a firm of travel agents in Braden, who's given him an alibi. The two of them were seen going into a cinema together a bit before the time Margot Weldon was killed and then having supper in the Ring of Bells. And as Laycock's got no car of his own, he'd have had no way of transporting her body to the common or running over it there. He might have borrowed Mrs. Silvester's car without its being noticed by her—apparently he sometimes did that—but Myra Bartlemy swears that he was on foot that evening and we've found a witness who saw the two of them arrive at the Ring of Bells on foot, without having to park a car outside it. So it looks as if we still have to look elsewhere for Margot Weldon's murderer."

"But if Laycock's got a criminal past of the kind you've just told us about," Andrew said, "he may have known someone quite unconnected with anyone else here who'd do the job for him while he was careful to set up an alibi."

"I thought you'd say that," Theobald said. "Just what I thought myself at first. And of course it's possible. If the person who did the murder and dumped the body then came on here to murder Mrs. Silvester, letting in that draught that you and she felt, it must have been someone who knew the ways of the house and Laycock could have told him about all that. But he did know you were here, Professor, as we've said before, which rather knocks that theory on the head."

"Yet you aren't sure he didn't kill her," Agnes said.

"That's true," he agreed.

"Why?"

"I've told Professor Basnett. Laycock heard Mrs. Silvester say she was going to change her will. He'd have realized what that would mean to all the other Silvesters, so he may have offered his services to one of them, or for all I know, to all of them, to make sure she hadn't time to do it. He'd have asked a high price for doing it. The diamonds, probably, would have been only part of the loot. This may be completely wrong, of course, but at least it suggests a motive."

The door opened and Laycock walked in.

"Police here?" he said, looking round the room with a smile. "And something tells me you may have been talking about me. Is there anything I can do for you?"

CHAPTER SEVEN

Nobody answered him. He stood in the doorway, looking cheerfully sure of himself. Yet, as the moments passed and nobody spoke, he began to look strained, as if an entrance that he had planned had not gone as he had intended.

"Well," he said to Theobald, his worn boy's face growing sullen, "don't you want to see me?"

"Very much," Theobald said, "but only if you're prepared to answer a few questions."

"I don't have to, you know," Laycock said. "I don't have to say a thing. And if you feel inclined to charge me with anything, I can call my solicitor."

"I'm aware of that," Theobald answered drily.

"If I answer your questions, it's only because I want to be helpful."

"Is that why you came back?"

"Why else should I have come?"

"Yes, indeed, why?"

"Go on, go on then. What d'you want to know?"

Something about the young man had struck Andrew the moment that he had started to speak. It was that he had dropped the kind of refined cockney accent which apparently he had thought appropriate to the role of Felicity's manservant and was talking with one which suggested a good education, probably a public school, perhaps Oxford or Cambridge.

Andrew was aware that a great many of the young these days are virtually bilingual, that they can talk the cultured English which was the normal manner of speech of their parents and which they themselves had spoken as children, but that whenever they feel like it they can adopt the accent of their contemporaries who have been less expensively reared. They do it usually out of self-defence, so that the people whom they would like for friends should not think them pretentious, but occasionally the ability to speak two utterly different versions of their mother tongue might have less innocent uses.

"I want to know why you went away on Friday," Theobald said, "and now, of course, why you've come back."

"I think you'd better come in and sit down, Ted," Agnes said. "You'll find there's a good deal to talk about."

He came forward and sat down, crossing one leg over the other.

"Mind if I smoke?"

No one answered, which he appeared to assume was permission to do so, for he brought cigarettes out of a pocket and lit one. Except that his self-assurance was perhaps a little overdone, he seemed perfectly at ease. He smiled at Agnes.

"Sorry about the way I walked out on you," he said. "You may have found it inconvenient."

"Don't talk like that!" she said with sudden anger. "You know the situation's terribly serious. It's not the time to be flippant."

"Sorry," he said again. "Yes. And of course that's why I came back, because it's so serious." He turned to Theobald. "Why did I go? That's the first thing you want to know, isn't it?"

Theobald nodded.

"Well, when you've a record like mine, which I suppose you know all about by now," Laycock said, "you don't like it much when you find the police under your feet all the time. From the time the Weldon woman's body was found and they started coming round here, I began to think of clearing out. But I might not have done it if it hadn't been for what happened on Friday afternoon."

"You mean when you heard Mrs. Silvester announce that she was going to change her will," Theobald said.

"No, no, what the hell had that to do with me? No, it was when I saw young Quentin making off with the old lady's diamonds."

"Quentin?" Agnes said sharply. "What d'you mean?"

"Just that," he answered. "I saw him coming out of Mrs. Silvester's room in a great hurry, stuffing something into his pockets. Then he dropped something and he stooped to pick it up and I saw it was a diamond ring. Then he went sneaking out as fast as he could and didn't know I'd seen him. I was standing in the doorway of Professor Basnett's room at the time—yes, yes, Professor," he added as Andrew was about to speak, "I'd been into your room just to see what you'd brought with you. I'm naturally inquisitive. But there was nothing rewarding there. I didn't really think there would be. And I was just coming out when I saw Quentin. So I waited till he'd gone, then I went into Mrs. Silvester's room and looked in the case where she'd kept her diamonds, and they were missing. And then I began to think about my own position."

"When did this happen?" Theobald asked. From the flatness of his tone it was impossible to tell whether or not he believed what he was being told.

"I can't tell you exactly," Laycock said. "Lateish in the afternoon sometime."

"After the Silvesters had left then," Theobald said.

"Oh yes, they'd been gone an hour or more. Quentin must have got away from them and come back on his own. I suppose he did it because he thought that if he and his family were going to be disinherited, he might as well make off with something tangible while he'd the chance and hope I'd be blamed for it. That's what I made of it at the time, anyway, and I thought it would be distinctly to my advantage to get away as fast as I could. I may have been wrong about that, but with that record of mine it seemed only to make sense. So I packed a small case I had and slipped out quietly and went to London. Does that answer your question about why I disappeared?"

"Not entirely," Theobald replied. "Why didn't you try to stop Silvester when you saw what he was doing?"

"And have him dump the diamonds out of his pockets and swear he'd been trying to stop me making off with them? Which of us d'you think would have been believed?"

"He'd have had to explain what he was doing there at that time of the day."

"Granted. But by the time I'd got that thought out, he'd gone. I could have told Mrs. Silvester about it right away, I suppose, but that would have done just the thing I wanted to avoid. We'd have had the place crawling with policemen and my record would have come out and I'd almost for certain have been sacked. So I decided I'd save her the trouble of doing that and discharge myself. Much less distressing than having scenes and accusations and all the rest of it. Besides, it doesn't come naturally to squeal on another chap. But perhaps you don't understand that."

"You're doing it now and you'd have done it right away if you'd seen any advantage in doing it," Theobald said. "I understand that much about it. What I can't say I understand is why you hadn't made off with the diamonds yourself. Evidently you knew where they were kept and you must have known their value and you could have got at them any time you liked. Why didn't you?"

Laycock puffed some smoke out languidly before he answered. "You won't believe me if I tell you the truth, so why should I?"

"Try it and see."

"Very well, Superintendent. The simple fact is, I've been going straight. You won't be able to find a single thing against me since my last spell inside. I did a lot of thinking while I was in there and I came to the conclusion there was no percentage in the way I'd been living. Going straight was the obvious thing. Not that I meant to stay in the kind of job I've had here for any longer than I could help, but you've got to start somewhere and it's one of the easiest sorts of job to get nowadays. But I meant to work my way up in time."

"But to get even a job like this one you needed a reference," Theobald said. "How did you arrange that?"

"Well, I got a friend to help me," Laycock said. "Girl who was an actress. Had the right sort of voice. She did it nicely."

"A girl?" Theobald said. "We've been told by the caretaker who let her flat to her that she was a middle-aged woman."

"That's right," Laycock said, but he looked disconcerted for a moment, as if he had been caught out making a slip. "One calls them girls, you know, out of habit. They don't want to be called middle-aged. That's natural, isn't it?"

"What was her name?"

He looked vague. "Can't remember. Let me think. Graveney, that was it."

"That's the name the caretaker had," Theobald said. "I want her real name."

"That *was* her real name, so far as I know. Sue Graveney. Only of course, she hadn't a title. We added that to make it sound better."

"What's her address?"

"I haven't the faintest idea. I haven't seen or heard of her since she did that little job for me."

"I don't suppose she really went to Canada."

"She may have, for all I know."

Theobald looked resigned. He was able, Andrew thought, to recognize a stone wall when he ran into one. Laycock might not mind incriminating Quentin Silvester, but at least for the present he did not intend to give away the woman who had helped him.

"So now we come back to the question of why you came back this morning," Theobald said. "And the truth would be a

nice change. Then you can come down to the station with me
and we'll have a written statement. If that will suit you."

Laycock grinned as if he had begun to take a liking to the
detective. It was a boyish grin, yet it had the odd effect of
making his round face look older than it did when he was
serious. It emphasized the little lines about his eyes and mouth
in a way that made them look as if they might soon become
permanent. He was at least thirty, Andrew thought, and a
hard-bitten thirty at that.

"I haven't told you a word that isn't the truth," he said.

"Perhaps only an odd one here and there," Theobald replied. "Now about turning up here this morning, why did you
do it?"

"Because I read the news in my paper about the old lady's
murder," Laycock said.

"Why should that have brought you?"

"Because the way it was put about the police wanting a man
to help them with their inquiries sounded pretty like me, so I
thought the sooner I came along on my own account the better. It's one thing to be suspected of stealing diamonds and
another to be suspected of murder. And it just happens I can
prove I didn't commit any murder."

"An alibi?"

"That's right. When I left here in the afternoon I went
straight to the station and waited around till there was a train
for London. Being Good Friday there weren't many and I had
quite a wait and I walked up and down the platform and had a
talk with the porter. I don't know his name, but he's the only
one they've got there and he'll probably remember me and
seeing me get on to the train when it came. Then when I got to
London I went to the room of a friend of mine, Charlie Lewis,
at 39 Grieve Street, and asked him if he could put me up for
the night. He said he could, then we went out for a meal at the
Black Horse, round the corner, and met some other chaps
there whose names I can give you if you want them and had a

few drinks, then went back to Charlie's and played poker for a time. Then the others left and Charlie made me up a bed on the floor and I was with him till I read the news in the paper this morning and decided I'd better come down. Anything you want me to add to that?"

Listening, Andrew realized that if this alibi that Laycock had given could not be shaken, Theobald would have to abandon his theory that Laycock might have returned to the house on Friday evening to murder Felicity by arrangement with one of the Silvesters. Yet all the Silvesters had alibis too, if they had told the truth about spending the evening together.

"All right," Theobald said. "You'd better come along with us now and give us a written statement. Any objections to doing that?"

"A pleasure," Laycock answered.

Agnes stood up abruptly. "Are you going to arrest him?"

"What for?" Theobald asked. "Concealing evidence? If he'd told us about seeing Quentin Silvester taking the diamonds, it might have been a help. On the other hand, it might have made no difference and it may not even be true. We'll wait and see. Come along, Laycock—if that's the name you're sticking to at the moment. We've a job of work to do."

The sergeant put a hand on Laycock's arm as if he thought that he might suddenly take it into his head to make a break for freedom, but he went apparently willingly with the two policemen. They let themselves out of the house and Andrew heard a car start up as the three of them departed.

Agnes had sunk down again in her chair. She sat crouched in it with her elbows on her knees and her face hidden in her hands. Andrew went to stand at the window, looking out at the lawn with its borders of daffodils and the big bush of forsythia at the bottom, glowingly yellow in the bright sunshine of the morning. It was Easter Sunday, he thought, and apart from its religious meaning, should have been a day for celebrating with rejoicing the return of the spring.

He remembered that when he had been a child his parents had always hidden a nest, full of chocolate eggs, somewhere in the garden, which he had to set out to find, and beside the nest there had always been a hare made of some material that had predated plastic, the head of which screwed off, revealing that the inside of its body was filled with chocolates. He had sometimes been puzzled by the problem of whether a hare could lay eggs or if its always being there beside the nest was a coincidence. Even now he was not quite sure of the accepted answer to the problem, though he guessed that Freud had provided one.

"Do you believe that?" Agnes suddenly asked. Her voice sounded muffled, as if she were struggling with tears.

Andrew turned and came back to the fireside.

"Believe Laycock? I don't know. Do you?"

"I meant that he saw Quentin take the diamonds."

"Knowing as little of them both as I do," Andrew said, "it's hard to say. I'm inclined to believe it."

"I thought Laycock had taken them," she said in a tone of strange desperation which made Andrew wonder suddenly if Quentin meant more to her than he had realized. "I was sure of it."

"It was a natural thing to think," he said.

"But Quentin—why should he do such a thing?"

"I think he's been badly wanting money recently, and even if he might have been ready to wait for it in the normal course of events till Felicity died, when she told the family she was going to disinherit them all, he thought he'd better make off with what he could while it was possible."

"But why should he specially want money?" she asked. "He's in a good job. I shouldn't be surprised if he's earning as much as his father. And Tricia's in a good job too. I suppose it's possible she may not want to go on working once she's married, but even if that's so, they'd be quite well off."

"She told me yesterday the engagement's broken off," Andrew said. "And the reason seems to be that as soon as Quentin comes into his money, he's going to give up his job and go to live abroad and start writing again. It sounds as if he really hates that good job he's got. But I believe he's had one try at writing already that wasn't very successful, and Tricia didn't seem to like the idea of his doing it again. She doesn't think he's got the talent to justify it. But if it's what he's very keen to do, you can see why he needs money."

"I see. You mean he took the diamonds simply so that he could give up his job."

"If Laycock's telling the truth about having seen him take them."

"Yes, of course it comes back to that, doesn't it?" She shook her head, as if she were trying to refute something that had been said to her, or perhaps it was only something at the back of her own mind that had not been put into words by anyone. "I was so *sure* he'd taken them himself."

"D'you know, you surprise me a little," Andrew said. "I thought you'd taken a liking to him. I'd have expected you to be pleased on the whole if it could be shown he's innocent of everything but getting into a panic and bolting."

She gave him a quick look which was one of the most despairing that he had ever seen on a human face. He could not understand it.

"Oh yes," she said, "I'm very pleased."

"You guessed he was a crook, didn't you?"

"Yes."

"But you wanted to help him if he was trying to go straight."

"Yes, yes, yes!" She leapt to her feet and shouted at him with the same sort of fury that he had seen in her once before. "And look what's come of it—murder! Why couldn't he have said he saw Quentin take the diamonds? The fool, the wicked fool!"

Stumbling, as if she could not see where she was going, she darted out of the room.

Puzzled and wishing that he had followed his own impulse the day before and returned to London where he could have been peacefully at work today on his notes on the life of Robert Hooke, Andrew left the room. But in his case it was to look for a drink. He found bottles and glasses in the dining room, helped himself to whisky and returned to the drawing room, wondering if lunch would be provided by Agnes that day or if he would have to satisfy his hunger as he had yesterday, with a sandwich.

Not that he ever had more for lunch at home than a sandwich, but when he helped himself out of the refrigerator here in Felicity's house he could not quite rid himself of the feeling that it was a kind of theft. Not on the scale of helping himself to her diamonds, but still a kind of stealing. He did not like the thought of being caught at it and hoped he would not have to do it again today.

To his relief Agnes presently returned to the drawing room and said that she had prepared some lunch, though she was sorry that it was nothing much. It turned out to be cold beef and a salad and bread and cheese. Her mood was subdued again. She seemed to be deep in her own thoughts. From time to time she made an effort to talk, but they spent most of the meal in silence. When it was over she said that she would make some coffee and Andrew returned to the drawing room. It was while they were drinking coffee that Laycock returned.

Before showing himself, he had changed into his white jacket and resumed the air of an impeccable manservant. Agnes looked at him helplessly as he stood in the doorway of the room, looking as if he were waiting for orders from her. It seemed to be too much for her. It was plain that she could not cope with the situation. Andrew did his best to come to the rescue.

"So they've let you go," he said.

"Yes, thank you, sir." The genteel cockney accent was back in place again.

"Why did they do that?"

"I couldn't say, sir."

"They simply turned you loose again?"

"Yes, sir."

"Without any explanation?"

"None at all, sir."

"Stop it, will you—stop it!" Agnes shouted at him, her voice rising as it did when one of her moods of fury was erupting. "Stop this playacting! Come in and sit down. Tell us what really happened."

Laycock came in, closing the door behind him. But instead of sitting down he went to one of the windows and stood there with his back to it. Perhaps he felt that even for a guaranteed ex-convict, rather than a mere servant, to sit down in the company of his employer would show too much familiarity. He groped in a pocket for a cigarette.

"Sorry," he said. The accent was gone. "It came automatically and I thought I might be a bit of use here. But if you'd sooner I didn't stay . . ." He lit the cigarette and blew smoke out lazily.

"What really happened?" Agnes demanded again.

"As I said, Mrs. Cavell, they just turned me loose," he answered. "I made the statement they wanted and was expecting to be held there for God knows how long when they seemed to get into a state of excitement and suddenly told me to go. I told them I'd be coming here unless you didn't want me to stay, and they made a note of it and that was that. If you don't want me around, of course I'll go right away. May I say, while I've got the chance, that I appreciate the kindness you and Mrs. Silvester always showed me, and I can assure you, in case you've any doubts, that I never touched a hair of her head."

She gave him a long, puzzled stare, trying to work out something in her own mind, but before she could speak the front door bell rang.

Still smoking and with an air of casualness that was new, Laycock lounged over to the door and went out.

It was Patricia who had rung the bell. She did not wait to exchange any words with Laycock, but thrust past him into the drawing room, looking wildly round it as if she expected to find more people there than Agnes and Andrew and that they would be sure to be doing something stranger and more dramatic than drinking coffee. There were the marks of tears on her cheeks, though she was not crying now. Her eyes were hard and bright.

"They've arrested him—Quentin!" she cried. "They came to the house and charged him and took him away. And the horrible thing is, I've been half expecting something like that to happen. He's been so strange, I *knew* there was something wrong with him. I didn't know what it was, and I tried to explain it to myself. I thought perhaps it was the effect his family had on him. But that didn't really make sense. And that he'd be *arrested*—I never even thought of it."

"You mean they've arrested him for the theft of the diamonds?" Andrew said. "Have they found them? Can they prove it?"

"The diamonds!" she said with derision. "Of course they found them. I don't believe he'd any idea what to do with them once he'd got them. He's such a fool. He's made one blunder after another. No, they arrested him for the murder of Margot Weldon and they've got absolute proof he did it."

After the moment of shocked silence that followed what she had said, Andrew observed, "Proof is a big word."

"Do you think I don't know that?" She turned away from him and walked to the window, standing there staring out into the garden. There was a terrible dejection in the slump of her shoulders. "I told you we'd broken off our engagement. Now I wish we hadn't. It feels hideously disloyal. But in any case, I'll stick to him."

"But the proof, what is it?"

"For one thing, a photograph." She turned to face Andrew. "They found the woman's address, you know, in her handbag, and they've been showing photographs of us all to her land-lady. They've been snapping us all at odd times, as you may have noticed. And the landlady recognized Quentin at once. She said he used to go to the room and sometimes stay there for days on end about four or five years ago. Then Margot Weldon gave the room up because she said she'd taken a job in the country, and that just about fits the time she came to work for Felicity. But then after a little while she turned up again and took another room in the building, but Quentin never went to see her any more. But now he's admitted he used to know her and that it was he who recommended her for the job here to his mother. And she remembered that all along, of course, and did her best to cover up for him, saying it was Max Dunkerley, but now she's broken down and just sits and cries."

"But that isn't proof of murder," Andrew said. "Isn't there any more than that?"

"Lots more. Don't you understand, it was Quentin who forged Felicity's cheques? Margot only cashed them at the bank. He needed money badly at the time, because he was trying to be a writer and he'd next to nothing to live on. And it was only when Margot was found out and dismissed that he got himself a job. But as soon as he'd got one, Margot started to blackmail him. She kept threatening to tell Felicity he'd done the forgeries and he paid her to keep her quiet. But then I came into his life and we even decided to get married, and that made him want to get rid of the past with all its threats and be free of that horrible load of blackmail. And that meant, you see, that he'd got to get rid of Margot."

"But this is all supposition," Andrew said. "It may be what happened, but is there any proof of it?"

She put both hands to her temples, thrust her fingers through her hair, stared at him as if he had said something preposterous, then dropped into a chair.

Her manner changed abruptly. In a quiet voice, she said, "He's confessed."

"To all this that you've been telling us?"

She nodded. "Not at once. But there are traces of Margot's clothing and some blood on the tyres of his car, so there wasn't much point in going on denying it. And the police had that photograph which showed he'd known Margot in the past, and they found out some facts about payments into her bank account which tally with withdrawals from his, and when all that came out he seemed to give up hope and told them everything. He told them he'd refused to go on paying blackmail and that if she'd come down here to see him, he'd make her a final payment and they arranged to meet in the late afternoon outside one of the pubs in Braden. I think she must have distrusted him, because she came to this house, didn't she, and almost made up her mind to come in, and I think that must have been because she'd decided to tell Felicity the truth about the forgeries. But she changed her mind and met him as they'd arranged. He'd got rid of me by then. I suppose he'd some plan for doing that, but as things turned out it was easy for him because we started out for a walk in the afternoon but the wind was so strong we turned back, and it happened I'd a headache and went upstairs to lie down, while he said he'd brought some work with him that he'd like to get on with. But really he went out to meet Margot and he drove her out to the common and strangled her there and dumped her body in the road and ran his car over it and planted the forged letter he'd prepared in her handbag, confessing she'd murdered Felicity."

"And then?" Andrew said.

"What do you mean—and then? Isn't that enough?"

"It's just that she didn't murder Felicity. But he came here to do it, didn't he? Somebody came. And what was the point of that confession if it wasn't going to happen?"

She gave him a distracted look and made a visible effort to control herself.

"Quentin didn't murder Felicity," she said.

"Not that evening," Andrew agreed. "Whoever came went away again. But what about next day?"

"Haven't you been told, we all spent the evening together? None of us could have done it."

"That's really true, is it?"

"Certainly it's true, unless she died much later than the police say. I suppose if she did, any of us might have slipped out in the night and killed her. But as it happens . . ."

"Yes?" Andrew said as she hesitated.

"Quentin and I spent the night together. He didn't go out."

"I see. In any case, it's unlikely she was killed later than we've been told. Agnes found the back door open about half past eleven, as if someone had just gone out that way, and we searched the house after it and found nobody. And she locked the door then, so if someone came later they'd have had to break in and I gather there wasn't any sign of that having happened."

Agnes, who had been sitting with her hands tightly clasped in her lap and her gaze moving swiftly backwards and forwards between Andrew's face and Patricia's, as if they were players in a tennis match, broke in, "And we were so quiet so as not to disturb Felicity! If only we'd looked in her room! I suppose it would have been too late to help her, but the police could have been on the job hours sooner and perhaps they'd have caught the murderer by now."

Patricia gave her a vacant look, as if what she had said meant nothing to her. She turned back to Andrew.

"Is there anything we can do?" she asked.

"To help Quentin?"

"Yes. That's why I came—to ask you that."

"Even though he's confessed he's a murderer?"

"Doesn't a murderer need help? Hasn't he a right to it?"

"He's made it rather difficult for anyone to help him."

"Couldn't he retract his confession?"

"But if it's true . . . You do believe it's true, don't you? He didn't make it up to shield someone?"

Her face brightened for a moment, as if this idea offered hope, but then the look faded. "No, it's true."

"The only thing I can think of," Andrew said, "is that we should get hold of Little and tell him what's happened. His advice will be much more reliable than mine."

"Felicity's solicitor, you mean."

"Yes, unless the Silvesters have another one."

"I don't think they have. Yes—yes, please, will you do that?"

Andrew went to the telephone and finding a book beside it in which the numbers most often used by Felicity were noted down, he leafed through it and found the number of Little, Little & Summers, which he presumed was the one he wanted. Dialling, he asked for Mr. Arthur Little and was put through to him.

Making it as bald as he could, Andrew told the solicitor that Quentin Silvester had been arrested for the murder of Margot Weldon and was at present in police custody. What, if anything, could be done about it he left to the lawyer. Arthur Little said that the first thing he would do was to get in touch with Dr. Silvester and find out what steps he had taken, and then, if Dr. Silvester wished it, he would go to the police station.

Putting the telephone down, Andrew told Patricia the result of his call.

He was interrupted by an exclamation from Agnes. "Look!"

She had got up from her chair while he had been at the telephone and gone to one of the windows. In front of the window there was a small round table with a vase of daffodils on it and beside the vase was a box of *papier-mâché,* inlaid with shell. It was open and Agnes was pointing at something inside it.

Andrew went to the window and looked at what was in the box. It appeared to be Felicity's workbox. There were scissors and a thimble and pins and needles and reels of cotton in it, but on top of these things there was a small, pale blue note-book.

"It's Felicity's address book," Agnes said. Her voice was hushed, as if the sight of it frightened her.

Andrew reached out to pick it up, but she put out a hand quickly to stop him.

"We oughtn't to touch it," she said.

"Why not?" He picked it up and began to turn the pages. On one at the end which had the word "Notes" at the top of it, he saw the name Graveney scrawled on it and a telephone number. He showed it to Agnes.

"Yes," she said. "But however did it get here? D'you think Felicity herself can have put it there? Accidentally, perhaps, and forgotten about it?"

"Do you remember if that detective who was searching for it yesterday looked in this box?" Andrew asked.

"I don't actually remember it," she answered, "but I should think he must have."

"Then it wasn't Felicity who left it here," he said. "Who else has had a chance to do it since he searched?"

She gave a grim smile. "You and me."

"No one else? I was out a good deal of yesterday afternoon. Did no one else come here?"

"Not that I know of."

"Was the back door unlocked as usual all day?"

"No, I thought in the circumstances I'd better keep it locked for the present."

"Has anyone besides you got a key?"

"I have," Laycock said.

Patricia started, as if she had been unaware of his presence in the room until he spoke. For the first time it seemed to strike her as curious that he should be there, casually leaning against the doorpost and smoking.

"But why should anyone return the book after taking it?" Agnes asked.

"It would be a rather bad thing to have found in one's possession," Andrew said. "And there was no point in keeping it once it turned out that Little had a note of Lady Graveney's name and number. But what made you suddenly open the box, Mrs. Cavell?"

She reddened slightly. "I don't know. It was just an impulse I had. That's true, even if you don't believe it."

Andrew did not believe it. He remembered that when Laycock had first returned from the police station, he had not sat down as he had been asked to do, but had walked over towards the window and stood there with his back to it while he said how much he appreciated the kindness that Mrs. Silvester and Mrs. Cavell had shown him. Agnes had seen him do that and perhaps had seen more than Andrew. Perhaps she had seen Laycock slip something into the box. But she might not have seen what it was and have been anxious to find out what he had done.

On the other hand, she might have put the address book in the workbox herself.

For the first time Andrew asked himself if it was possible that Agnes had killed Felicity.

If she had, it had cost her a fortune. If she had waited only a few days to do it, she would have found herself a very rich woman. Always supposing that she had got away with it. But as it was, she had gained nothing, whereas a number of other people had gained a great deal. A number of people, all of whom had alibis and could not possibly have committed the murder. Whereas the people who had no alibis had no motives either. One of them had already confessed to committing another murder, as well as forgery and deceit. Was he just the single offshoot that had gone wrong of a family that was otherwise law-abiding and honorable? Or was there something rotten at their root?

Felicity herself had believed that no one who knew her had cared for anything about her but her money, and perhaps that very belief had brought into being the state of affairs that she had derided. She had responded to all kindly advances with suspicion. She had given no affection in return. She had actually taught her family to think of her only in terms of the money that she would leave them. Thought of in those terms, it might be said that she had brought her murder on her own head.

All the same, which of them, Agnes or Laycock, had put the address book into Felicity's workbox? And why?

Had Patricia been near the workbox since she had come into the room?

Andrew remembered suddenly that she had, but while he was still trying to reconstruct in his own mind what her movements had been since her arrival, the front door bell rang again.

As before, Laycock went to answer it and brought Frances Silvester into the room. Her wispy hair had a dishevelled look, as if a wind were blowing, yet outside it was calm and still. Her small face, which had probably once been pretty, was tense with pain. She ran to Agnes and threw her arms round her neck.

"Agnes, what am I to do—tell me! You always know what to do," she cried. She bent her head on to Agnes's shoulder. "He's confessed, but he didn't know what he was saying. I'm sure he didn't know what he was saying. He can't have meant it. He can't have done what he said he did. You don't think he did it, do you?"

Agnes remained oddly stiff in the other woman's embrace.

She patted her on the head, but looked past her as if her mind were on something else.

"Professor Basnett rang up Mr. Little," she said, "and he said he'd get in touch with Derek. I think that's all any of us can do at the moment."

"But don't you understand, Quentin didn't do it!" Frances wailed. "It must have been someone else in her life who did it. A woman like that—God knows how many people she's ruined or driven mad. Someone followed her down here, don't you see, and killed her where it would look as if one of us had done it."

"And put that forged letter in her handbag, confessing to a murder that hadn't happened?" Agnes said. "It must have been someone who knew an awful lot about us all."

"But then what can I do for him, Agnes? I've got to do something."

"Wait to see what Mr. Little advises."

"Oh dear, you're so sensible, but I don't think you understand what I'm going through. That poor boy!"

"He chose to confess, didn't he? No one beat him or tortured him. And the fact that he confessed may help him and so may the fact that he's been paying that woman blackmail for years. I should think that may be looked on as an extenuating circumstance."

"But they'll send him to prison. They'll keep him there for years."

"At least they won't hang him."

Frances gave a little squeal of horror. She withdrew several steps from Agnes.

"I believe I've been quite mistaken about you," she said. "I don't believe you've got a heart."

"Perhaps not one in the best condition," Agnes answered. "I'm sorry, Frances, but hysteria upsets me. To help Quentin now you've got to keep very calm and sensible."

The door bell rang again.

"Oh, God, who is it *now?*" Agnes demanded with a trace of the hysteria in her voice that she had just criticized in Frances. It was one of the moments when the strain of the last days appeared to be too much for her. "Why can't they leave us alone?"

Andrew half expected that it would be Theobald, but in fact it was Derek and Georgina. Theobald, he supposed, was otherwise engaged at the moment, going step by step through Quentin's confession, making sure that he was in fact the forger and murderer that he had claimed.

False confessions, Andrew believed, were often made to the police from a variety of motives, from the unusual one of desiring to protect the person who was really guilty, to the commoner one of simple exhibitionism. But thinking of the smooth young man whom he had seen here before Felicity's murder, who had her pale golden hair, her blue eyes and her fine features, as well as her vividness and the charm that she could always exert when she chose, Andrew was surprised to find that it was easier to think of him as a dishonest and cold-blooded criminal than as either quixotic of pathetically perverse.

Derek strode into the room ahead of Georgina, ignoring everyone but Frances whom he caught hold of by the arm and pulled round to face him.

"What are you doing here?" he demanded. "Why did you suddenly go driving off like a maniac?"

"I wanted to talk to Agnes," she answered. "Agnes is always so wise. At least I thought so, but I'm not sure about that any more. I'm not sure about anything. But I knew you wouldn't listen to me. You never listen to me. You always treat me as if I were a fool. But I'm not a fool. I'm only liable to get a bit muddled about things sometimes, and then when you shout at me like this I get worse."

"You're a fool and a liar," he said. He turned to Agnes. "What has she been telling you?"

"Oh, no lies," Agnes said. "Only things you might expect from any mother."

Frances gave a sigh, extricated her arm from Derek's grip and sat down. "What I've been trying to say is that Quentin may not have been the only person Margot Weldon was blackmailing, so he may not be the only person with a motive."

Derek nodded sombrely. He patted her on the shoulder, as if he regretted having been so harsh with her. "I'm afraid we've got to accept it that he's done what he said," he said. "I don't understand how a son of mine could have got himself into such a position. He had a good home, a good education, he knew Frances and I would always give him anything he wanted within reason. He'd only to ask for it."

"Within reason!" Georgina suddenly yelled. She had sat down on the arm of her mother's chair and had been absent-mindedly stroking her hair. "He only asked you for anything once. He asked you if you would give him a small income for a year or two so that he could see what he could do as a writer. And you told him a writer who had anything in him wouldn't have to be dependent on his parents. You told him to get a job and do his writing when he had the time."

"And I'd do the same again," Derek said bitterly. "And no doubt he'd do the same again, forge his grandmother's cheques or somebody else's, because that's how he's made. But I'll tell you one thing. I'll spend every penny I get from Felicity defending him. I'll get the best lawyer I can and do everything humanly possible to get him a light sentence. I dare say it won't be possible, but I'll try."

"And how much better it would have been if you'd given him the money to lead the life he wanted," Georgina said sneeringly. "Then none of this need have happened."

"It would have happened sooner or later," Derek said. "That streak of crookedness was bound to come out, just little by little at first, the odd cheque now and then when he thought he could get away with it, but getting reckless till he was caught. And perhaps eventually leading to murder as it has."

"You don't want to take any of the blame yourself," Georgina said. "You think you can buy yourself off now by spending money defending him, but you know you should have given it to him when he asked for it."

"I don't know anything of the kind," Derek answered violently. "He was old enough to stand on his own feet—as you are yourself, my child. Drifting from one thing to another without any sense of responsibility and coming home in betweenwhiles when it suits you isn't going to get you anywhere. But you've just been waiting for Felicity's money, haven't you? That's what you've both been doing. And you all but wrecked your chance of getting it by your foolery with those diamonds. If someone hadn't stepped in to make sure she hadn't time to change her will, you wouldn't have got anything. You haven't only a murderer for a brother, but a murderer for a very kind friend."

Georgina had grown pale while he had been speaking.

"That's a horrible thing to say!" she cried.

"That's right, it's horrible," he answered. "And what a pity it is you can't change your parents for ones you'd like better, just as I wish at the moment I could change my children for another pair."

"Please, please," Frances said, her eyes filling with tears. "Don't talk like this. It doesn't do any good. And you don't mean what you're saying, either of you. Let's go home." She stood up and turned with an unsteady sort of dignity to Andrew. "These family rows don't mean anything, you know, Professor Basnett. I'm sorry you've had this one inflicted on you. We're all so quick-tempered, but we always end up making peace. Derek and Georgina are really very fond of one another. Come along, both of you. We'll go home."

She put an arm through Derek's and he let himself be guided to the door.

Georgina, with a sullen look on her face, lingered as if she were not sure that she wanted to leave with her parents, but then she strolled out after them. Patricia hesitated, then followed them too.

As the door closed behind them Agnes let out a long breath.

"I know I ought to be sorry for them," she said, "but I'd prefer it if they did their quarrelling elsewhere."

"Do they quarrel a lot?" Andrew asked.

"I don't really know," she answered. "I've always suspected they weren't a very happy family, but in front of Felicity they were always careful to be very sweet to one another. Actually she'd have enjoyed watching them quarrel, but I don't think they understood that. Well, I must go and see what there is for us to eat. I had such nice meals planned for your visit, Professor, and you just haven't been getting them. But I'll see if I can manage something tolerable now."

"Please don't go to any trouble on my account," he said. "My appetite isn't at its best."

She smiled at him. "That's probably true of us all, but I'll see what I can do."

She left the room and Laycock followed her out.

Andrew walked about restlessly for a few minutes, glad to have the room to himself and grateful for the quiet in it. But he was disturbed by a feeling which came to him all too often nowadays that he had forgotten something of importance, something which he had been on the verge of expressing a short time ago, but which, just before he did, had been completely washed from his mind. Something had interrupted him, no doubt, something possibly of no importance. But he knew from experience that the harder he tried to recapture what he had lost, the more elusive it would become. The only way to do it was to get his mind off it completely, then there was a chance that it would suddenly return to him as clearly as if he had never forgotten about it.

Because he did not want to think about the matter, whatever it was, he fell back on muttering to himself the rhyme that had kept taking possession of his mind recently.

"When all the world is young, lad,
And all the trees are green;
And every goose a swan, lad . . ."

Something checked him. Hadn't Felicity said something about her swans quite often turning out to be geese? He thought he remembered her saying that, and believed he had reflected at the time that Felicity's swans of the moment were obviously Agnes Cavell and Edward Laycock. But Agnes had succeeded in remaining a swan for four years, which surely was long enough for any gooselike qualities to have revealed themselves, whereas in Laycock's case it had been a matter of only four or five months. After spending five years in prison.

Five years is a long time.

But in some circumstances four years can be a long time too. A long time to wait. A long time in which to feel lonely. Almost as long as five years . . .

Abruptly Andrew stood still. The thought that had been eluding him suddenly yielded itself to him. And it meant that there was something that he ought to do. Ought to do immediately. The sooner the better.

Going to the telephone, he picked up the directory and looked for the number of the police station. When he had dialled and a voice answered, he said who he was and that he would like to speak to Chief Superintendent Theobald. After a brief wait he heard Theobald's voice.

"I've thought of something that may be important, Mr. Theobald," Andrew said. "I think you should get in touch with the Department of Molecular Biology at the University of Derby and find out what they can tell you about the family of a man called Eustace Cavell. In particular, was there a son—"

That was the last thing he knew. Something crashed on his head. Pain and shock blinded him and a thought flashed through his mind before darkness came that this was death. Then he fell in a heap on the floor.

CHAPTER EIGHT

It was not death. Not, that is to say, unless it was to be expected that the first thing that he should see on being resurrected was the face of Chief Superintendent Theobald. The face of the superintendent, kind, concerned and more than a little curious, hovered above Andrew as though in a dream. Then the darkness closed in again.

When it lifted once more he had no idea of how long he had been unconscious. He had no sense of time. It might have been for minutes, it might have been for hours. But above him he could see the ceiling of Felicity's drawing room and he was aware that under him there was something very hard. So it seemed probable that it was the floor and that he had not been moved since that moment of which he had a faint recollection when something had descended on his head. For a moment fear possessed him. Had they left him lying there on the floor because they were afraid to move him. Had his skull been fractured? Had his neck been broken? Was he dying, if not dead?

Experimentally he tried moving his head and felt a hand immediately laid on his forehead. There was something soft under his head, a cushion perhaps.

"Take it easy," a voice said.

"Have they gone?" he asked, or thought he asked. His voice sounded to him so distant that he did not think it could be audible to anyone else.

But someone answered, "It's all right, we've got them."

That was satisfying, though for the moment he was not sure why.

"I don't understand . . ." he began to say.

The other voice said, "Don't worry, there's an ambulance coming. Probably not necessary, but it's best with concussion not to take any risks. We're packing you off into hospital."

"Have I got concussion?" Andrew asked.

The face of Theobald swam into view above him once more. He was smiling an amiable but sardonic smile.

"That's all," he said. "I believe he stopped her killing you, according to our men. Quite a risk you took, phoning the police with a murderer loose in the house. Another time you'll know better."

"But how did you get here so soon? I'd hardly begun telling you what I was going to say."

"We have our methods. No reason for you to concern yourself."

After that Andrew found that it felt very comfortable to close his eyes again and let himself drift back into darkness, which no longer seemed frightening—only restful.

He had no memory afterwards of being lifted into the ambulance or taken to the hospital. When full consciousness at last came back it did so with odd abruptness. A man in a white coat, presumably a doctor, was standing by his bed, talking to a nurse, and all of a sudden, out of nothingness, Andrew heard him say ". . . really remarkable."

That was all, but Andrew at once felt sure that the doctor and the nurse were discussing the fact that it was really remarkable that he should be alive. All the same, he felt that there was something ridiculous about having been put into hospital simply because he had had a knock on the head. Not that he could remember ever having been hit on the head before. He had really led a very sheltered life, he thought. Even during the war, being a scientist, he had been in what had been called a "reserved occupation," and though he and Nell had

had to sit through their share of air raids, the only trouble that they had had was when their front door had been blown off its hinges by the blast from a V-2, and that had happened at a time when they had both been out of the house, so they had not been frightened by it.

A memory of those far-off days came back to him and he thought of it with a kind of pleasure before letting the doctor see that he was conscious. It was of himself standing in a bus queue with two stout, elderly women in front of him, both of them with shopping baskets on their arms in which, no doubt, they had been collecting their rations. And one had said to the other in a tone as matter-of-fact as if she had been talking of the weather, "The one thing I don't like is being machine-gunned."

"Look, he's coming round," the nurse said. "He's smiling at something."

The doctor bent over the bed. "Well, how are you feeling, old man?" he asked.

"Old, as you say," Andrew answered. "Very old indeed."

"Now I didn't mean—"

"Never mind. But I'm feeling my age. How long am I supposed to stay here?"

He noticed that there was darkness outside the window, so he supposed it was still the same evening as the one on which he had lost consciousness, not the next day.

"We'll see about that," the doctor said. "Meanwhile, is there anyone you'd like us to get in touch with and tell them you're here? Any friend or member of your family?"

"Why, am I dying?" Andrew asked.

"Certainly not. I just thought if you've a wife or children or anyone else—"

"I haven't." Andrew's only relation was his nephew who at present was in Paris, busy writing the science fiction which made him a far ampler income than Andrew had ever achieved in his scientific career, and he saw no reason why he should interrupt these remunerative activities. "Is it true they've got those people?"

The voice that had told him that they had seemed hazy and unreal now, perhaps only part of a dream.

"The young man and the woman?" the doctor said. "I believe so. But that's not my business. How do you feel about talking now? Superintendent Theobald wants to talk to you as soon as you're up to it, but I can fend him off for a bit longer if you'd prefer it."

"I'd sooner talk to him, I think," Andrew said.

"All right, if it's going to set your mind at rest. But not for too long."

The doctor and the nurse went out.

Andrew realized that he was in a private ward, a small room with the usual paraphernalia of a hospital in it and he wondered who would pay for it. The police, since it would have been at their orders that he had been put there, rather than into a general ward? Or would the bill be presented to him? In any case, he was glad to be alone and not to be the object of the curious glances of the other occupants of a big ward, which would certainly have been concentrated on him once the police came visiting.

A few minutes after the doctor had gone, Theobald came quietly in. He drew up a chair to the bedside and sat down.

"You're a lucky man, Professor," he said, "but I expect you know that by now."

"I suppose so," Andrew said. "Did I get it right that your men arrived in time to see the man stop the woman finishing me off? Or was that just something I imagined when I wasn't quite with you?"

"No, that was quite right."

"But why were your men there? I asked you that before. You didn't explain it."

"I told you, we have our methods. But it almost seems, doesn't it, as if your mind and mine have a way of working along the same lines, even if our approach is different? Now let me ask you a few questions. When did you begin to suspect Laycock was Mrs. Cavell's son?"

"I can't say exactly. It was something that built up little by little that there was some close connection between them. To begin with, it was only that she was always on his side, trying to defend him if anyone criticized him. Then there were various things that all came together when it suddenly occurred to me that the time she'd been working for Mrs. Silvester was about the same time that Laycock spent in prison. Not that that would have meant anything by itself if I hadn't realized how easy it would have been for her to get Laycock the job in Ramsden House."

"But I thought that was one of the problems," Theobald said. "That Mrs. Silvester had engaged him independently when Mrs. Cavell was away on holiday. There seemed to be no connection between them."

"That's what I thought until I had a conversation with Mrs. Godfrey, the woman who's been coming in daily to clean for the last ten years," Andrew said. "She told me it was Mrs. Cavell who put the idea of employing a manservant into Mrs. Silvester's head. And also she said that Mrs. Cavell found some advertisements from people who wanted that kind of job and tried ringing them up, but didn't find anybody who'd suit. Then she went away and almost immediately afterwards Mrs. Silvester saw one of these advertisements herself and rang up and managed to engage Laycock on the spot and was very proud of having done so. Well, wouldn't it have been very easy for Mrs. Cavell to have left a newspaper with a few of these advertisements in it where Mrs. Silvester would see it, and with the ones she'd already tried, or said she'd tried, crossed out, and just the one remaining that gave the number of Lady Graveney? And what would be more natural then than for Mrs. Silvester to ring up that number and talk to that nice Lady Graveney, who of course was Mrs. Cavell, disguising her voice, and be told that Laycock was everything that she could possibly desire? And Mrs. Silvester did honestly believe she'd engaged him herself without any prompting, because she liked to feel independent and didn't realize for a moment that the whole thing had been set up for her by Mrs. Cavell."

"Lady Graveney was described to us by the caretaker of the flat where she stayed as a middle-aged woman with black hair," Theobald said. "Mrs. Cavell is grey-haired."

"Easily covered by a wig," Andrew said, "or perhaps she just made do with what I believe is called a rinse. I believe, unlike a dye, it washes out quite easily, though I'm not very well up in such matters."

"Quite so." Theobald had not needed to be told that, but his face showed that he was deeply interested in the working of Andrew's mind. "And you believe, I assume, that it was Mrs. Cavell who extracted Mrs. Silvester's address book from her handbag after the murder, because she knew there was a note of the Graveney number in it. But she didn't know at the time that Mr. Little had a note of the number too."

"Yes, and that was another part of the puzzle that fell into place. It was after it came out that he had the number that she began to get scared. I had a curious scene with her which began after your detective had searched the bureau in the drawing room for the address book and failed to find it, with her bursting into tears, which I naturally took to be caused by her grief for Mrs. Silvester. But she denied it and said it was because of her violent disappointment that she wasn't going to inherit Mrs. Silvester's money. And I believed her, but of course it wasn't true."

"You aren't telling me it really was grief."

"Of course not. And I don't believe now the tears were real. She did a great deal of noisy sobbing and mopped and rubbed her eyes, but I can't swear to it that I saw any actual tears. No, what she wanted to get into my mind was that she'd wanted the money very badly and that she was the one person who'd really lost by the murder. We've all been hypnotized in this case, I think, by the belief that 'the love of money is the root of all evil.' Of course that's totally untrue. It can be a relatively harmless foible. But everything to do with Margot Weldon's murder, everything to do with the Silvester family, was connected with the love of money. So that's how we thought of Mrs. Silvester's murder too, instead of recognizing that there are other loves that can be far more dangerous and destructive. Sad to say, maternal love is one of them. I thought of that when I heard Frances Silvester trying to defend her son."

Theobald nodded thoughtfully. He had not been watching Andrew while he had been talking, but had his head propped on one hand. Now he gave him one of his swift, perceptive glances.

"Is this a bit much for you?" he asked. "Shall we give it a rest and have another go at it later?"

"No, let's get on with it,' Andrew said. "Let's get it over. But before we go any further, will you tell me how your men came to be on the spot when Mrs. Cavell attacked me?"

"Oh, we hadn't been nearly as penetrating as you," the detective answered. "It's just that we've got resources that weren't at your disposal. As a matter of routine we investigated the background of everyone who had any connection with Mrs. Silvester."

"Including mine?"

"Of course. But up to the moment we haven't come up with anything to your discredit, whereas in the case of Mrs. Cavell we discovered that there'd been a son who'd given trouble since his childhood."

"She told me she hadn't any children and I believed her at the time."

"Naturally she'd say that. The facts about him, so far as we could discover, were that he'd run away from home twice before he was twelve, then disappeared completely when he was fifteen and after about a year was discovered working in a travelling circus. I think he may have been happy there and if he'd been left alone, he might have stayed fairly straight, but he was sent back to school and, being a bright boy, got into Cambridge. But he didn't stand that for long and disappeared again,' after which his parents appear to have given him up. But later he took to turning up from time to time with stories of how well he was doing in films—perhaps he really did for a time; there's a bit of the ham actor about him, isn't there?— and so on. But at least some of that time he spent in prison. There were one or two minor offences for which he was given short sentences, but then there was the bank holdup in Croydon in which one of the clerks was badly injured and Laycock got five years for that. And it was when that happened that Mrs. Cavell came to work for Mrs. Silvester. I imagine it was because she was lonely and that the last thing she'd have dreamt of at the time was that it would end in murder. But when Laycock came out she made a desperate effort to save him. She got him the job here, where he would be under her eye. And for the time being at least, I believe he was intending to go straight."

"But she couldn't bring herself to trust him," Andrew said. "That was the trouble, wasn't it? When the diamonds were stolen she took for granted he'd taken them. She told me so."

"She really did that?" Theobald said. "Now that's interesting."

"She didn't exactly mean to do it," Andrew said. "But after Laycock told you he'd seen Quentin take the diamonds, she was talking to me and she gave me one of the most despairing looks I've ever seen on a human face and told me she'd been *sure* Laycock had taken them. It puzzled me, because, as I said, until then she'd always done her best to defend him. And now suddenly she seemed to want him to have been the thief. And of course she did, because if he wasn't, she need never have committed murder. She'd just discovered that she'd done something brutal and horribly unnecessary and I think it nearly drove her crazy."

"You were in the house when she did it," Theobald said. "Didn't it strike you that anything unusual was going on?"

"I'm afraid I'd fallen asleep," Andrew said. "I just dozed off in a chair by the fire and didn't wake up till Mrs. Cavell came to tell me that someone had left the back door open."

"Having opened the door from inside herself, of course."

"Yes, and I ought to have thought of that much sooner than I did. She was so intrepid, going round the house. It was her own suggestion that we ought to search it, then she went from room to room without the slightest sign that she was afraid someone might jump out at her with a lethal weapon. Of course she knew there was no one there. She merely wanted to impress on me, perhaps because she saw I was still groggy from sleep, that someone had come in from outside."

"About her being so sure Laycock had taken the diamonds," Theobald said, "when did you come to the conclusion that protecting him from the consequences of the theft was the motive for the murder?"

"I think I was uneasy about it from the start," Andrew said, "though I didn't understand it. It was just that after Mrs. Silvester had gone up to bed she suddenly called Mrs. Cavell up to her and she sounded very excited. I know I expected some sort of rumpus to break out, but in fact everything was quiet. And that's when I fell asleep. And later Mrs. Cavell told me that Mrs. Silvester had wanted her simply to assure her that she'd meant what she'd said about changing her will and that Mrs. Cavell was really going to inherit everything. I didn't question it, though I felt there was something strange about Mrs. Silvester having sounded so excited when she called Mrs. Cavell upstairs if it was only something like that that she wanted to say. But she was altogether in a very excited state that evening, so I didn't think much about it. Of course what she really wanted to tell Mrs. Cavell was that the diamonds had been stolen."

"And she assumed Laycock had taken them?"

"Yes."

"And Mrs. Cavell saw all the effort she'd put in, trying to redeem her son, going to waste, and silenced Mrs. Silvester before she could call the police. Even if her son was guilty of the theft she didn't want him arrested again and perhaps getting an even longer sentence than before."

"Yes, you said yourself a woman could have strangled someone as old and frail as Mrs. Silvester, and Mrs. Cavell's quite sturdy and has good strong hands. I remember noticing that when I first shook hands with her. I suppose she stopped Mrs. Silvester crying out by putting a pillow or something over her face. Using strangulation then may have been an attempt to make it look as if it was connected with the other murder, which at first it was thought to be. Anyway, by the time it happened, I was probably asleep. I expect they talked for a time, Mrs. Cavell trying to persuade Mrs. Silvester that Laycock might not be guilty, or perhaps to give him another chance, but Felicity was a very stubborn woman and if she'd made up her mind to call the police, she'd have done it."

"And after the murder Mrs. Cavell took the address book out of Mrs. Silvester's handbag, hoping that she could prevent any connection between her and Laycock being traced, then opened the back door and woke you up. You know, don't you, that the address book turned up in Mrs. Silvester's workbox?"

"Yes, and it was that that made me think seriously for the first time that Mrs. Cavell might be the murderer. It had not been there, I assumed, when your detective searched the room, and since he'd done that the only people who could have put the address book into the workbox were myself, Mrs. Cavell, Laycock and Patricia Neale. I knew I hadn't done it, but I was witness to the fact that both Laycock and Patricia Neale had gone to the window and stood close to the little table with the workbox on it and might have slipped the address book in while I wasn't looking. But why should either of them have done it? The book would have been a dangerous thing to have found in one's possession, but returning it to the workbox was dangerous too and there was no need for either Laycock or Patricia to have done that. They'd both been out of the house and could have disposed of it anywhere. But Mrs. Cavell had been stuck at home since the time of the murder and could have found it difficult to get rid of the book. She may even have had it hidden on herself all the time your men were searching for it. And she probably thought it would look better if she appeared to find it than have it discovered by one of your men. She wasn't afraid that Laycock would be suspected of having planted it, because she knew by then he'd got an alibi and was quite safe, but Patricia might have been a useful suspect."

"How she must love that boy," Theobald commented. "If only he'd been worth it!"

"I remember thinking there was a great power for loving going to waste in her," Andrew said, "but I didn't realize how tragically to waste."

"What a surprise it must have been for Quentin Silvester to find that someone had committed the murder of his grandmother for him," Theobald said. "And how fortunate for him that he failed to do it the evening before, because, d'you realize, he hasn't gained in any way by her murder, so when he's done his time for the murder of Margot Weldon he'll find a nice nest egg waiting for him? He'll quite legally inherit all his grandmother left him, with accrued interest."

"Really?" Andrew said. "I suppose he will. I hadn't thought of that."

"I'm rather glad there's something you haven't thought of," Theobald said, "though it's been a pleasure talking to you."

"I'm still not clear how your men happened to be on the spot when Agnes Cavell attacked me."

"That was just luck. As I told you, we found out the probable connection between her and Laycock and a couple of men
went to Ramsden House to bring them both in for questioning.
We'd nothing solid against either of them yet. And my men
happened to hear you yell, saw Mrs. Cavell attack you with a
poker and so of course they broke into the house. Laycock was
trying to hold her back. She was practically out of her mind by
then, but he's a professional. He's economical in the use of
violence."

"It's funny, I don't remember yelling," Andrew said. "I just
remember darkness and silence."

"That's common enough when you get a blow on the head.
You've remembered a lot more than a good many people do
who've had concussion. And thank you for filling in a lot of
details we hadn't sorted out, even though we'd got the main
outlines. But you're looking very tired. I'd take your time before trying to leave here if I were you. Don't hurry to get back
on your feet."

As any normally healthy person does in a hospital, Andrew
determined that he would get back on to his feet at the first
possible moment, but for that evening at least, when Theobald
had said good-night and left him, it was pleasant enough to lie
still and be ministered to by a young nurse who clicked her
tongue at him disapprovingly and said that at his age he
should know better than to get into such trouble, but who
smiled while she said it, and who presently gave him a pill to
swallow, the purpose of which she did not tell him, but after
taking which he sank into a deep, quiet sleep. He slept without
dreaming until he was ruthlessly woken in the early hours of
the morning by a woman with a cup of tea. For once he completely forgot that he liked to start the day with a piece of
cheese.

He stayed in the hospital for two days and during that time
he had two visitors.

The first was Mrs. Godfrey. She came, bringing him a bunch of daffodils from her garden and voluble condolences. He was not sure if it was mainly compassion or curiosity that brought her. Probably it was a mixture of the two, he thought, in which case it must have been a disappointing visit for her, for even though Andrew was glad to accept her sympathy and her flowers, he became very vague when she questioned him. After his long discussion with Theobald, when he had talked almost compulsively, he had lost all desire to talk to anyone else. He denied having any more knowledge of the case than she had herself, most of which, he gathered, she had gleaned from the newspapers. For though she had had one or two dramatic interviews with the police, just enough to make her want more, she was in general bewildered. She had an idea that something that she had told him was central to the investigation, but she did not understand what it was. Perhaps it was not kind of him, but Andrew explained, with some truth, that he still had a terrible headache and that he found it very difficult to think clearly.

His second visitor was Max Dunkerley. He was in his sweater and corduroy trousers with a leather jacket and with his scanty pinkish hair curling on the roll collar of his sweater. He sat down in a chair by Andrew's bed, fastening his wide-open, startled eyes on his face and saying nothing. Andrew mumbled something about it being very good of him to come, but did not know what else to say.

At last Max Dunkerley remarked, "I'm getting her pictures, you know."

"Yes, I supposed you'd have them," Andrew said.

"But I haven't thought about hanging them yet." Max said it in a tone of defiance, as if he expected to be criticized for it.

Andrew remembered the walls in Max's flat, already covered with pictures.

"Well, there's no hurry about it, is there?" he said.

"The fact is, they'll remind me of the whole bloody business and I'd like to forget it."

"That will take some doing, won't it?"

"Oh, I don't know. You can make yourself forget most things if you try hard enough."

Andrew thought of how he had been pursued throughout his life by trivial verses, memorized in his childhood, which he would have loved, though without success, to forget.

"Perhaps I've never tried hard enough," he said.

"For instance, I can forget nearly all the time that I ever asked that woman Agnes to marry me," Max said. "What a mercy she wouldn't have me, though I was very put out at the time. But just think what it would have been like finding oneself lumbered with a stepson like Edward Laycock."

"I suppose it would have been unfortunate."

"Apart from other disadvantages there might have been." Max sat musing for a little while. Then he added, "Poor woman."

Andrew was not certain if he was referring to Agnes or Felicity, but did not inquire.

Max fell silent again, his gaze now bypassing Andrew's face and fixing itself on a spot on the wall of the ward.

"I'm thinking of selling the pictures," he said. "Do you think there would be anything wrong about doing that?"

"I should say it's entirely up to you," Andrew replied.

"The fact is, I can't help feeling guilty when I realize I'm benefiting by Felicity's death. I wanted those pictures so much, you see. I used to think sometimes I wished she'd hurry up and die so that I could have them. And that seems terrible now."

"If you sell them, you'll still have the money you get for them, unless you give it to a charity," Andrew said. Somehow he could not see Max giving the money to charity.

"But there's something abstract about money," Max said.

"It isn't tangible, like a lot of pictures you're looking at every day."

Andrew had heard money called a great many different things at different times, from a "good servant" to the "sinews of war," not to mention the "root of all evil," but he thought it was the first time that he had heard it called "abstract."

Max explained, "It gets lost so easily in the housekeeping, doesn't it? When I drink a bottle of whisky, I shan't think I'm drinking Felicity's lifeblood."

"I'd wait and see how you feel about it in six months' time," Andrew said.

"Yes—yes, I'm sure that would be wise. Well, I hope you make a good recovery. Perhaps if I'm in London one day, we might have lunch together."

Andrew said that that would give him great pleasure, though he felt fairly sure that the invitation would never be issued. If Max went to work as hard as he had said at forgetting everything that had happened that Easter, he would quickly forget Andrew.

He discharged himself from the hospital next day though he still had a very sore patch on his head and felt somewhat shaky. He had been told that he would be required to attend both inquests, but he thought that he would sooner spend the time before them at home than at the Ring of Bells. He had to return once to Ramsden House, into which he was taken by a constable, to retrieve the few belongings he had left there, and the sense of desolation it gave him made him want to leave it again as quickly as he could. At the railway station of Braden-on-Thames he bought a copy of the *Financial Times* and settled down to read it on the short journey home. But he could not concentrate on it. Closing his eyes, he fell into a half doze till he reached Paddington.

When he reached home the April sun was in a kindly mood, the sky was blue and the almond trees along the sides of the street were in gay and delicate blossom. Letting himself into his flat, he kicked off his shoes, left them lying in the middle of the room, padded across it in his socks and switched on the electric fire. As he did so he caught himself chanting a rhyme to himself. He chanted it aloud, as there was no one there to hear him.

"Spring, the sweet spring, is the year's pleasant king,
Then blooms each thing, then maids dance in a ring,
Cold doth not sting, the pretty birds do sing . . ."

He welcomed it because it was so completely divorced from the grim Easter that he had just endured. He knew that by the time it had hammered away in his head for two or three days, as it probably would, he would be deadly bored with it, but at least for the moment it charmed him. He was not sure who had written it. Not Shakespeare, but certainly one of the Elizabethans, not one of the more banal Victorians, and that, he thought, gave it a certain status. Pouring out a glass of whisky, he settled down once more to the *Financial Times*.

About the Author

E. X. Ferrars lives in Oxfordshire. She is the author of over forty works of mystery and suspense, including *Something Wicked, Death of a Minor Character* and *Skeleton in Search of a Closet.* She was recently given a special award by the British Crime Writers Association for continuing excellence in the mystery field.